*C*ome (hands
Silas and Kota both appeared at the doors and stepped out. They tried to look casual but they were walking double time and went right for the car. Silas climbed in back with me; Kota took the front seat.

I turned, putting my knees in the seat and facing backward to look out the rear window, watching for any sign of Greg or his friends.

"Are they out there?" Victor asked.

"I don't see them," I said.

"I think we lost them," Kota said, sounding breathless, leaning against the seat.

"Sang, I think we're safe. You can sit," Silas said. His finger jabbed me in my side. Unfortunately, it was the side that was bruised and I wasn't expecting it. I winced and cried out an ouch before I could catch myself.

Silas's eyes widened. His large hand pushed me back up against the seat. He lifted my blouse away from the top of my skirt. Cool air caressed the bruise and I shivered.

"Where did that come from?" he demanded.

"I..."

He let go of me, turning his body to face the door. His hand clutched the handle. "Turn the car around."

"Silas," Kota started.

His fists clenched and he spoke through his teeth. "I said turn it around."

The Academy

The Ghost Bird Series

Introductions

♥

Book One

♥

Written by C. L. Stone
Published by
Arcato Publishing

From The Academy

The Ghost Bird Series

Introductions
First Days
Friends vs. Family
Forgiveness and Permission
A Drop of Doubt
Push and Shove
House of Korba (Fall 2014)

The Scarab Beetle Series

Thief
Liar (Summer 2014)

***

Other Books by C. L. Stone

Smoking Gun
Spice God

ACKNOWLEDGMENTS

Thank you, Terese, for beta reading and being awesome.

Thank you, Chrystal, for putting me on the path for the best thing I've ever done. Writing will forever be different for me.

Thank you, Karin, for being the best cheerleader ever.

Thank you, WPLH, and all friends for putting up with our craziness – Monday through Weekend Warrior Days.

Thank you, Chad, for putting up with my obsessions.
(Turtles!)

.

♥

MAX

My heart thundered under my breast. I was sure my parents could hear me, asleep in their beds inside the two story, gray-siding clad house on Sunnyvale Court.

Rain puddled at my feet, soaking the dirt of a thousand walks into my off-brand tennis shoes. I usually enjoyed the rain. I liked the feel of walking barefoot through puddles in the grass and the smell of rain mixed with pine trees. Tonight, the rain was cool and the air crisp against my skin for early August in South Carolina. I would be out all night, though, so this was completely bad timing.

With my toes pointed out to the street, I stood at the edge of the long driveway. A cool wind split through my dark poncho. I wanted to shiver, but I steeled myself and ignored the cold.

This is it, I told myself. *If you're going to leave, you need to do it now.*

A new house sat half-finished around the bend of Sunnyvale. I'd explored it yesterday while on a walk and discovered the back door was unlocked.

My hand gripped the straps of my overloaded backpack. *One night,* I told myself. One night where I'm not sleeping under the same roof as my parents. *I'm not going to die, like my mother seems to think I would.* Normal people, everyone else in the world, weren't all murdered and raped the moment they went outside.

Thoughts of my bedroom in the house behind me

flooded my mind: the soft green comforter, the mauve carpet, the warmth of the cotton sheets, a quiet symphony playing from the stereo. I shook my head at the thought, lifting a hand to my brow to flick away the collection of water there. No. I had already made the decision. Besides, it was too late to turn back. Sneaking out of the house was hard enough to do at night. I wouldn't want to be caught trying to sneak back in.

I forced my leg up and out to step foot on the dark pavement of the road. My parents' house was the newest on the half-circle street, tucked away behind a forest near a new highway. There were only twenty homes in the neighborhood. In front of my parents' house was an empty lot with room for one more house, but the land was still undeveloped. The rest of the street had several middle income homes and made for a very quiet neighborhood. Unfortunately, the street light was never installed in front of my parents' home. Even though I knew the blacktop was flat, it made me nervous that I might trip on a stick -- or an ax murderer.

I stomped my other foot onto the road, turned left and started walking. The wind swept up around my face, and I tucked my head down to brace myself against it. I fell into the deeper shadows of the road, shielded from the glow of neighbors' outdoor lights. I shivered as a breeze picked up around me.

Even as my heart continued to pound, I moved forward. Every second I envisioned my sister or my parents waking to find me gone and glancing out the window to spot me. Only I knew better. They probably wouldn't notice until well into the afternoon that I was nowhere around. The reluctance I felt was only the whispers of my mother echoing in my head.

A slippery thudding sound started racing toward me. It was so soft at first that I thought it was my own heart. The sound drew closer. I imagined some maniac running barefoot toward me. I stared out into the dark, trying to use the light from the house further up the road to catch whatever it might be. *I should move*, I thought. *I should get out of the way.* I

2

willed myself to turn around. A gust of wind swept into my face. My eyes watered.

A mass hurled itself at me and I fell back. My book bag slipped away from my body and I crashed onto my butt and my left arm. My hand and wrist scraped against the street. Something heavy and wet sat on top of me. A warm, salty breath filled my nose.

My wild imagination ran through every possibility. Rapist. Murderer. The instinct to scream swept through me but my throat caught and I only gasped. I was paralyzed.

A slobbering tongue licked my arm and then a soft, cold nose nuzzled it. My heart continued to beat but I finally took a breath, relieved.

"Hey," a shout came from up the road, from the direction I had been heading. "Are you okay?"

My whole body went rigid again. The sound of footsteps came closer and I tried to angle myself out from underneath the dog, but it wouldn't budge and instead continued to sit on my legs. It barked and then licked my arm again.

"I'm sorry," said the voice. "Max, get off of her." In the shadow of the street, I couldn't tell who it was. I wasn't that familiar with the neighbors anyway. The voice was smooth, masculine. While his tone was gentle, there was a strength hidden behind it. Since he wasn't shouting at me or telling me he would kill me, I tried to calm my heart.

They're not as bad as she thinks, I told myself. People aren't all evil.

The dog was pulled away from me. The guy knelt by my side. An arm went around my shoulders, lifting me slightly. "Are you hurt?"

His touch around my shoulder sent a shiver through me that I couldn't control. It was such a warm gesture and I wasn't used to people touching me. Through my shivering, I felt the pang at my hip where I had fallen. Pain seared through the scrapes on my arm. I coddled it to my chest. "I'm okay," I said through my teeth. "It's fine."

"No, you're not," he said. The strength in his voice

shining through more. "You scraped your arm." He put another arm around my waist and prepped his knees. "You can stand, right?"

My cheeks flushed so hot, I could have been glowing. As much as I felt awkward, I was scared to admit that this stranger's kind hands on me felt so reassuring. "I think so."

He pulled me up gently with him until we were standing together. The wind whipped around us. My poncho flew like a flag behind me. He turned his body until his back was against the wind, protecting me from the worst of it. He brought his hands up to cup around my face. "I'm going to take you to my house."

It was the first time I noticed the glasses. The light from up the road reflected in them. I still couldn't guess his age. From what I felt of his body, he was easily a head taller than me and there was some definition to his muscles.

I blushed at the thought that I had been touching his chest.

He bent over and picked up my book bag. He grunted at first as he lifted it.

"Let me take it," I said.

"No." He heaved it over his shoulder. He wrapped his free arm around my shoulder and guided me up the street. "Let's get out of this rain. We'll assess the damage inside."

"What about your dog?"

"He'll follow."

My heart pounded again as I followed him up the street. My hands shook, my knees quivered. I tried to think calmly, that this was just him being nice. My mother's voice shot through my head, all her warnings swirled through my mind.

I could only hope I wasn't on my way to die.

KOTA

*H*is house was the first one on the right after the empty lot. I remembered seeing it from my bedroom window. It was a one story, brick, ranch-style home, with a finished room over the two-car garage. The garage door was open, with one car parked inside. Another car was parked in the corner of the wide driveway toward the back. A safety light flicked on automatically as we crossed into the garage, revealing the green poncho he wore. The hood covered most of his face. If I had seen that coming toward me in the night, I would have run, screaming. I wondered if it was wise now to follow him into his house.

The dog followed us then sat by a crate which was leaning against the wall. He waited, wagging his tail. In the shadows, he looked so big, and I could smell the heady wetness of his fur, making my nose tickle.

"Not now," the guy said, waving his hand at the dog. The dog sank to the floor, head on top of one of his paws. The guy hit the button for the garage door to close. The light went out, sinking us into complete darkness, blinding me.

"Come on," he said. He took my uninjured arm and pulled me inside. I stumbled in behind him.

Once we entered the house, there was a short hallway with a wood floor at our feet. The house was dark and I crept along behind him, keeping close to his back, afraid of getting lost. I caught a glimpse of a dining room beyond the hallway. Before we got to it, he opened a door to the left, just before the end of the hall. It opened to a stairwell, with light blue carpeting covering the steps. A dim light shone from somewhere above.

He started up the stairs. I didn't know if I should follow, but I didn't want to be caught downstairs if there were other people in the house.

Imagining that we were alone in the house also scared me.

I followed him up. At the top, the bedroom above the garage was spacious. There was a door open to the left that led to a small bathroom. Another door next to it was closed and I guessed it to be a closet. There were windows facing the driveway and one looking out onto the road at the front of the house. The window toward the front had a bench seat with a couple of neatly embroidered pillows in the corners. A bed was pushed up against the wall leaving a huge amount of space in the middle. In the far left corner was a computer desk, monitor turned off. A small bookshelf sat next to it.

A brass lamp glowed on his desk. He crossed the room, touching it a couple of times and the brightness increased. He turned to me.

His black-rimmed glasses had droplets of moisture, slightly masking his eyes and almost hid his high cheekbones. His light brown hair stuck to his forehead and at the top of his ears. If I had to guess his age, he might have been a couple years older than I was, if that. He was a head taller than I was, with a medium build and his skin was fair. The way his thin brows angled at the edges made him look curious and constantly interested. His poncho had a Nike swoosh mark and his black Converse shoes looked brand new. If my older sister would have seen him, she would have told me he was a nerd right off. She may have missed the way he was standing upright, shoulders back, with a cool confidence that I could only dream to have. What etched into my mind, though, was the kind smile he had on his face. It warmed me instantly.

I blushed when I realized he was examining me under the same scrutiny. I imagined I looked like a complete wreck. My dark blond hair was tied up in a small bun in a clip, but

6

half undone and sticking to my neck. My small nose was probably bright red from the surprising chill of the night and my green eyes were probably bloodshot or had heavy bags or both. I was probably as pale as a ghost with the dark poncho sagging around me. My jeans were sticking to my legs, my Sketcher sneakers were discolored from wear and dripping.

"I'm sorry," I said. "I should probably have taken my shoes off. They're soaked."

"I'm not worried about the carpet right now. One thing at a time." He dropped my book bag on the floor by his desk and then moved toward the bathroom door. "Take that poncho off and let's look at your arm."

The bathroom had just enough room for the tub, a toilet in the middle and a counter for a sink to the left with a wide mirror above it. The powder blue flowery wallpaper and a matching set of rugs made it feel cozy.

I followed him, pulling the poncho away and bending over a little to pull it off of me. The green t-shirt underneath stuck to my body so much I might as well not have worn it at all. It was up against my breasts, even pushed up between them, clearly outlining the details of the underwire in the bra I was wearing. The cloth sucked into my belly button.

His eyes followed where I was looking. I tried pulling the shirt away from my body but as soon as I let go, it fell back against me, attaching itself to my skin. His cheeks tinted red as he took the poncho from me and hung it on the shower curtain rod.

He reached over for my left arm lifting it gently. In the light, I could see blood had dripped over my wrist from a gash. I sucked in a breath. Now that I was focused on it, the pain in my arm burned and throbbed.

He lifted my arm closer to his face investigating the cut, using a gentle push of his forefinger to see if it was still bleeding. "My god," he said. "I'm sorry. Really. This was my fault."

I shook my head at him, trying to look nonchalant about the pain. "It was your dog. Not really his fault. He was excited, I guess."

7

"He was excited," he agreed. He moved away to open a drawer under the counter. He lifted out a red and white first aid kit, and reached for a bottle of hydrogen peroxide. "I've noticed the lead was getting thin in the middle for a while. When he smelled or heard you, he took off and it broke." His eyes met mine as he tugged me gently closer by the elbow so that I would be at a better angle for the light. "He's not usually that bad. He needed to go out but he hates this weather. So, I'm sorry about that. I should have replaced the lead before now. And I don't know why he jumped on you. He never does that."

His eyes were emerald green and with the light from above us, or maybe it was the way his glasses were hanging a little lower on his nose, I felt my breath escape me. I found his eyes to be gorgeous. From the depths of my mind, even while distracted, I knew I was supposed to say something, but the way he was looking at me made my heart skip and my mind went blank. I wasn't even sure why I felt the way I did. I only knew that he was making my insides flutter. "...name."

A brown eyebrow arched. "Hm?"

"I don't know your name."

The soft lips smiled at the corner, just enough. He was pleased with me. "I'm Kota."

Kota. It was different, like mine, so I liked it.

He waited patiently for a moment and then chuckled, as if uncomfortable. "What's yours?"

It took me a moment to guess what he meant. My head was still foggy, so following the conversation was difficult. "Uh... Sang."

"As in, I sang a song?"

I nodded. "I know it's weird."

"No weirder than 'Kota'."

I smiled a little. "I suppose not. Weird names are nice, though."

The crest of his high cheekbones tinted to a pink that looked nice on him. "It's nice to meet you. And please don't hate me."

"For what?"

He applied a clean cloth with the peroxide to my arm. I had been so distracted by him that I hadn't noticed he had prepared one. The sting went straight to my bones. The chill I was still feeling from the weather outside only made it that much more uncomfortable. A shutter ran through my body, wracking my bones together, causing the sting to radiate through me. I bit my lip, holding back the urge to cry out in pain.

As he cleaned my arm, I turned my head, looking out into his bedroom. Not watching him not only relieved the pain but also the awkwardness I felt. I wanted to look at his face but I was too nervous to face him, and didn't want to get caught staring.

After the blood and dirt were washed away, he applied a large square bandage to cover the spot. "I think you're patched up." He gave the sides of the bandage a few more rubs to ensure they were sticking and then crumpled the plastic wrapper in his hands. "Anything else broken or bleeding?"

I shrugged and shook my head. I didn't want to mention my hip, which felt very sore. It wasn't bleeding, so I didn't think it was important to mention. "I'm fine."

He looked at me a moment, as if wondering whether I was being honest with him or not. He slowly nodded. "Okay. Well, Sang, I hope this won't ruin your impression of me right off."

"What do you mean?"

"I mean we are neighbors, right? Your family just moved in?"

My eyes widened. I guessed there was no hiding it. "Yes. No. I mean, don't worry about it. It was just an accident." I pursed my lips, unsure if I should say anything more.

His forefinger moved to the bridge of his glasses and he slid them up. The muscle in his forearm flexed. "So what were you doing out so late?"

I had been hoping he wouldn't ask. "Just taking a walk. I couldn't sleep."

"With a book bag weighing a ton on your back? In the middle of this weather?"

My face heated up and I didn't know how to answer him. The silence stretched on between us as I struggled with words. I stalled for so long that I didn't know if I could respond at all.

A sympathetic, but confused, smile spread over his lips. "Hey, I'm sorry. Look, it's personal. Whatever it was, did you have to do it in the middle of the night?"

I sucked in a breath. "It felt like a good idea at the time."

The corner of his mouth dropped slightly but he caught it and his face relaxed and became unreadable. "Okay. Here's what I'm going to do. I'm going to find you something dry to wear. I'm going to go downstairs to change. I'll make some hot chocolate, too. If I come back and you're not here, I'll understand. If you are, you get to tell me what's going on." His head bowed a little until his forehead was so close to my own that I could feel his warmth from it. I had nowhere to look but into his beautiful green eyes. "I make a halfway decent friend, if you give me a chance."

I didn't know how to respond to this either, so I simply nodded. A complete stranger was offering his friendship. Right here, in this moment, it was something I never imagined. I felt my eyes watering and I turned my face away from him to hide it. I couldn't look into his eyes any more. It was like he could see into me and who I really was, and I didn't want him to see me.

He straightened up and stepped out into his bedroom. I stood in the doorway of his bathroom to watch. He opened the closet and pulled out a gray t-shirt.

"It'll be big on you," he said. He dug around into the back and pulled out a pair of blue striped pajama bottoms. "These might be too big as well but they at least have a tie." He hung the clothes over his arm and closed the closet door. I stepped backward into the bathroom and he held out the clothes. Our fingers brushed and his eyes held mine. "Just put your wet things in the bathtub for now. When they aren't so soggy, we'll toss them into the dryer."

I was unable to express to him how warm and welcome he was making me feel. I mustered up my warmest smile. It was all I could manage.

When he spotted it, he paused in his motions to look at me. I wondered if I appeared crazy to him, so I tried to backpedal and look just normal -- pursing my lips and looking compliant.

There was a change in his expression that I didn't quite understand, but he turned away and closed the bathroom door behind himself.

After he left, I flipped the lock on the door and stood in the bathroom, looking at my reflection in the mirror. My hair was strung out, even though the clip I had it twisted in hung on. My cheeks and nose were red and my skin looked so pale in comparison. I felt embarrassed that he saw me like that. The thought of leaving crept into my mind. This was more than I was prepared to handle. Spending a night out was one thing. Staying in a house with a boy pushed thoughts into my head, whispers my mother would recite to me. Rape. Sexual assault. Kidnapping.

Only Kota had shown more warmth and caring toward me than I'd felt from anyone in a long time. Here was proof against everything my mother had taught me about the dangers of the world. The first person I'd met took me in, was making hot chocolate and was inviting me to be his friend.

My heart was pounding at the thought of him coming back. Despite his warmth, despite my own head telling me this was just what people did, that normal people were nice and helpful, I was still nervous at the thought of him knowing anything about me.

Was it better to be alone?

♥♥♥

I put on his shirt and pajama pants. The ends of the waist tie hung to my mid-thigh after I tied it off. I rolled the cuffs on the pant legs but my heels were still stepping on the cotton material. I didn't want to be in the bathroom when he got back, so I tiptoed into his bedroom.

The desk was so neat, it looked brand new. The bed was unmade but the corners at the foot were tucked in sharp angles. He must have gotten up to take out the dog. The sheets were calling to me, but I was too uncomfortable to sit on his bed, and I was too sore to stand. I moved to the window seat and knelt on the cushion to look out.

Rain splattered against the window. In a way, I suppose I was lucky to have run into Kota. I picked a bad night to break into an empty house. Why hadn't I considered the weather when I'd thought to do this? I knew the answer to that, though. Earlier that day my mother had made a point to lecture me as I was doing the dishes.

"There was a little girl on the news today," she had said, standing across our kitchen and watching as I rinsed plates. She had her arms folded under her heavy breasts, bulking up the material of her thin burgundy robe. "Three men kidnapped her from her front lawn and molested her. It took only a minute."

It was one of a hundred similar stories I had heard over the week. I had to bite my tongue to stop myself from telling her there were millions of girls who played on front lawns that weren't kidnapped. It wouldn't matter. She wouldn't listen. It was so overwhelming to me. I felt I needed to prove it to myself. It was my way of bringing myself into reality and not getting swallowed up into the nightmare she insisted was true. One night out of the house would be enough.

"I guess you're staying," Kota said behind me. I turned on the bench seat to look at him. He was wearing a clean white t-shirt and a pair of green pajama bottoms. His brown hair was combed away from his eyes. He carried two navy blue mugs with steam spiraling off the top. "I hope you're good with marshmallows."

I smiled. Who didn't love marshmallows?

He tilted his chin toward me. "Scoot over."

I tucked my knees into my chest and moved toward the

window, my back pressed to the wall. Kota took the outside, his back against the opposite wall, and handed me the mug. The warmth from the outside of the cup was a little too much for my still chilly hands, so I held it carefully by the handle with my fingertips barely touching the bottom. Blowing gently to cool it, I took a sip, letting the warm, sweet liquid pool over my tongue before sliding down my throat.

"So where did you move from?" He took a sip from his own mug, but his eyes fixed on me.

I blushed and glanced out the window. "A tiny town in Illinois."

"Did you leave any friends?"

I shook my head and turned back toward him. "No one I would write to. I really wasn't that close to anyone."

His hands rubbed at the mug, his thumb tracing the lip and he cast his eyes to the marshmallows floating on top. He had a knee up on the cushion of the window seat. His leg was just a breath away from mine. The almost-touch made my heart flutter. "You'll be going to the public school, right?"

Why did he say it like that? "Like everyone else, I guess." For which I was grateful. Despite my mother's complaints about sending us to school, my father insisted we were allowed. It was the only thing he stood up to her about. I believed he was sure if we didn't go to school she could never keep up with a home school system and the state would be after them.

Kota looked up, confusion in his face. "What grade?"

"Sophomore," I said. I hoped it was okay to be honest.

His head tilted, his eyes sparked. "Me, too. What are you going to take this year?"

I shrugged. "I don't really know what I want."

He blinked. A silence stretched between us. We sipped our cocoa together and my eyes flickered between his knee that was so close to mine and the window. It was a strange feeling, like something I had seen out of a movie. Two people sharing an evening together and dabbling with small talk. Did people really do things like this? My mind whirled with something to say, but I was never good at starting conversations.

After a few moments, he spoke. "Do your parents want you to take something in particular?"

I sighed and nodded. "The daughter of an electrical engineer should have a degree in something. My older sister already started in the arts. I'm getting pushed into science."

"Would it be that bad? Science is pretty awesome."

I grimaced. I didn't want to insult him by being honest. I liked science but I wasn't sure if it was my favorite. "I don't know if I want to do that."

His head tilted as he gazed down at me. "What do you prefer?"

"I'm not sure, really," I said. Thoughts of the paperwork in my room filled my head. I liked this conversation better. It didn't feel too personal. "There's so many choices. I don't know if I want to devote my life to science. Or art. Or something else. It all sounds good."

He laughed softly. "That sounds familiar."

I blushed again because I didn't understand what he meant. I moved the mug up to my lips, mostly to feel the heat from the cocoa. "I don't hate science. I don't hate anything. It's like I want everything. Not fully. I just want a touch." I was rambling and took a sip of cocoa just to get myself to shut up.

He fiddled with his own mug. "Sang... where were you going?"

I kept the mug close to my lower lip and breathed deeply, letting the warm sweet air fill my lungs. "There's that new house up the road. I was going to sleep there for the night."

"You were running away?"

I closed my eyes. I hated those words. "No. Not for forever. I just wanted one night out of the house."

"So you wanted to break into a house? Alone? In the middle of the night?"

My face burned and I turned my head away to look out into the night again. Only this time the sight was blurred by tears. "It sounds crazy." I blinked a lot, trying to force the tears back. When I felt a little calmer, I turned again to look at him. "I wasn't going to hurt anything. My parents are... different. I don't get out much. I just wanted to get away for the night. I didn't want to feel trapped anymore."

"You just needed a release."

My heart lifted. He understood! "It was just a bad night to do it. I probably shouldn't have thought of the empty house. I just knew the back door was open and I wouldn't have harmed anything."

The corners of his mouth lifted. "I have to admit, I can't imagine you committing a breaking and entering. You don't look like the bad girl type."

I made a face at him and he laughed. When he did, I couldn't help it and giggled too. "I guess it seems pretty silly. It's just a single night."

He tilted his head. "Why tonight? I mean, what happened today that you felt you had to get out?"

I blushed again and I held a palm to my cheek, pretending to rub it so I could hide the redness. "It's complicated."

"I'm pretty smart. Try me."

Now that I'd said all this out loud, it did seem dramatic and silly. "It seemed a better idea than hiding away forever. I don't want to believe the world is all that terrible." My voice shook as I spoke. I worried that I might cry in front of him.

His smile softened and his eyes sparked again. "Sang, you're an idiot."

The insult made my mouth pop open and a rush of heat radiated from my face. "But... I..."

He lifted a hand and dropped a finger on my open lips to stop me from talking. "Three reasons. For one, you picked a bad night to take off."

I couldn't disagree with him. I also couldn't think clearly. His finger remained on my lips and I wasn't sure how to move. It was hard to concentrate on what he was saying.

"Two, if you knew the house was empty, someone else could be lurking in there, too. Maybe a hobo or some other

15

teenagers. It might not be true of you, but people who break into houses are often not very nice people. You'd be walking in on them."

I hadn't even thought about that. "What's the third?" I asked, even as his finger was still on me and I was more than mumbling. He grinned and moved his finger away.

"If your parents caught you, you might have been grounded for a lifetime and I would have never met you."

My heart stopped in that moment. I thought he was just teasing me, but something in his eyes shimmered honest. It melted me at the core. He cared. About me? But why? How?

He tilted his mug and drained the rest of the cocoa. "Do you have to be somewhere tomorrow?"

I shook my head.

"Are you still intent on staying out for the night?"

Would he tell my parents about it? Somehow, I didn't think he would. He was giving me a choice. Did I really want to do it? He was right about not going to the empty house. Walking out in the middle of the night was not the best way to prove anything other than I was taking a big risk. However, I couldn't stand by and let myself be caught forever in the small world they built for us. "If I could figure something else out..."

He put the mug down and then planted a palm on my knee. "So how about this, I'll let you sleep here tonight. I think you'll feel better in the morning about it all. After that, give me a month."

It took everything in my will power not to pull away from his touch. It felt so intimate that it made me shake. I blinked at him, confused. "To do what?"

"We'll get your parents to relax so you don't have to sneak out."

I smirked again. "Now who is being idiotic?"

He smiled, sincere and warming. "I mean it."

"You don't know me. Why do you care?"

He shrugged. "Friends help each other. We're friends now, aren't we?"

I couldn't answer him right away. Could it really be that

simple? Growing up, I wasn't allowed to attend parties or even just hang out. Outside of school, I saw no one. Friends were the people I sat with at lunch. I never said a word to them otherwise, never called, never went to the mall with them. The truth was I didn't have a clue what a real friend was supposed to be like. Was friendship supposed to happen so quickly? "I suppose so."

He nodded and then stood up, taking my mug from me. "I'm going to take these downstairs and put Max into his crate. You go hop into bed."

My mouth fell open and I glanced at his bed. "But... you..."

He laughed at my expression. "Don't worry. There's a roll-away bed underneath that one. When I get back I'll pull it out and will sleep there."

My parents would have a fit. Still, I shivered with excitement. I'd never been out anywhere and my first night away from them, I would be sleeping in a boy's room. "But maybe I could sleep on the roll-away thing. I mean, it's your bed."

"Just get in, will you? It's late." He turned and thudded his way back down the stairs.

I froze where I was for a moment. Again, tears came to my eyes. He was so nice to me. How could I leave now? Maybe he was right. Would he keep his promise though? Could I trust him? I'd already told him so much and I couldn't believe I'd admitted out loud what I had never told a soul. It was those green eyes and the way he looked at me. He made it so easy to talk to him, because he was so calm and he instantly knew what to do. It was almost like magic.

I fidgeted with the hem of his shirt as I stepped toward his bed. I swallowed thickly, trying to still my heart. Forbidden territory. I inched myself down, sitting carefully on the edge until I heard it creak. Was I afraid it would bite me? I think I was more afraid of my parents somehow finding out.

Only they wouldn't find out.

I tucked my toes in between the sheets, relaxed my head

onto the pillow and yanked the blanket up over me. With the blanket pulled up to my chin, my body warmed a few degrees. I hadn't realized how cold my body was before. When my bones thawed, my whole body melted into the bed. I inhaled a delicate scent, a spicy fragrance. Is that what he smelled like? The softness of his pillow forced my eyes shut. Kota's bed. A boy's bed.

The next time I opened my eyes, the room was dark. From what little light came through the window, I could see the roll-away bed that had been pulled out. Kota was on his back, his elbow against his forehead. His mouth was open and he was breathing slowly. With his glasses off, he looked completely adorable. I stayed awake as long as I could to watch him.

My new friend.

♥

VICTOR

I dreamed about fire in a house I didn't recognize. I was running to find a door, knowing someone was chasing me but I couldn't see his face. I didn't want him to find me. I didn't want to burn.

My eyes popped open the next morning when sunlight managed to filter through the sheet I had over my head. I worried I would drool or something and Kota would laugh. There was a chill and I pulled the blanket over my head. I pushed the corner up an inch to peek out. I didn't want to get up if he was still trying to sleep.

I wondered how awkward he must have felt having a strange girl sleep in his bed.

Kota wasn't there. Neither was the pull out bed. How early did he wake up in the mornings? Usually I was a very light sleeper, so it surprised me he could get up without me hearing him. I wasn't sure what to do, so I rolled onto my back, covering myself with the blanket fully and waited. I didn't want to get up and poke around without him. *That is clever of me*, I thought. *Too scared to get up when he's here. Terrified when he isn't.*

Time passed for so long I thought maybe he'd forgotten about me. I turned on my side to face the wall, trying to will myself to relax and just get up and face whatever was downstairs. I was just getting myself to sit up, when the sound of a door opening broke the silence, followed by thudding at the stairs.

I fell back onto the bed, and pulled the blanket over my head to cover my face, trying to feign sleep. I wasn't sure why I did that, but it seemed like a safe thing to do to pretend to wake up while he was nearby.

After the thudding ended on the stairs, there was only silence. What happened? I held my breath underneath the blanket. My ears strained to hear any sound. Was he being quiet to let me sleep? My heart thudded against my chest, loud, and I wondered if I would hear him at all. Should I get up now? Was he doing something? I was tempted to take a peek, only I wasn't sure if he'd notice.

"Hey Kota!" A male voice called out, clearly trying to be loud on purpose. There was something striking in the voice though. Smooth. The baritone was like a familiar singer but I couldn't remember the name. "Still sleeping? What's wrong with you?"

A body landed so hard on top of me that I felt the air in my lungs escape, robbing me of enough oxygen to cry out. Legs fell over mine, someone's frame sat on top of me and hands sought out my wrists under the blanket. I managed to let a muffled grunt escape, but with the way he held my arms, my face was stuffed with blanket and I couldn't twist myself free.

"Are you getting up or what?" The voice said, the baritone playful. "The world is spinning on without you."

"Victor." Kota's voice came from the other side of the room. I hadn't heard him come up.

The person on top of me froze and then let go of my arms. The blanket was yanked away. My arm jerked in quick reaction, shielding myself from the sudden onslaught of light and from the stranger sitting on top of me.

"Who..." Victor never finished his statement. His mouth hung open.

His brown eyes were wide, big, and it was the first time I'd thought the term "fire in his eyes" ever actually fit a face. The intensity would have made me blush in any normal situation, but as I was in a bed and he had just landed on me, I was glowing with heat. His head flinched back in confusion and I was just as dumbstruck. His body was slighter than Kota's and he looked like he was the same age we were. His hair was a softer brown, reaching to the nape of his neck in gentle waves, brushed back away from his eyes.

"Victor, this is Sang."

Victor blinked at me repeatedly. "Uh..." He moved off the bed and stood up. He wore a crisp white long-sleeved shirt, the top button undone to reveal the start of his collarbone. He wore neat black slacks. His near formal attire surprised me, but he appeared comfortable in what he was wearing, like he wore it nearly every day. At his neck hung a silver chain with a round silver medallion with some symbol I didn't recognize. His face was angular. His hips were slimmer than Kota's and his fingers were long and lean. "What are you doing here?" he asked. "I mean, in his bed?"

"She slept here." Kota held a smile on his face and wore a calming expression, as if this was perfectly normal. He was wearing Levi jeans and a light blue Polo shirt with a collar, the buttons done up all the way to the top.

Victor spun on him, his hands shooting out, palms up. "Are you kidding me?"

"Don't get weird. And don't tell my mom. I don't think she'll understand."

"But *why* is she..."

Suddenly a voice called up from the base of the stairs. "Kota? Do I hear Victor up there?"

Before Kota could reply, there were footsteps coming up. I panicked, wondering if I should jump from the bed.

Kota took one look at Victor and they both reacted at the same time. Kota headed to the stairwell, standing at the top. Victor came to the bed, pushed me back so I was lying down and covered me with the blanket. He positioned

21

himself in front of me, sprawled out. I couldn't see him from under the blanket, but I could feel his body near mine and it caused me to blush.

I did my best to make myself as small as possible.

"Yes, we're up here," Kota said.

"Hi, Victor."

"Hi."

"I thought you boys could come down for breakfast. It's almost ready."

"Mom," Kota said. "Is it okay if I let Sang stay for breakfast, too?"

"Sure. Who's Sang?"

"She's the girl from next door. The family that just moved in."

"Oh..." Pause. "Where is she?"

"In the bathroom."

"She came in with me," Victor added.

"Sounds good. Have her come down. I made eggs."

The sound of footsteps on the stairs trailed away. In a flash, Victor hopped up and pulled the blanket away from me. When he did, he looked me over and tilted his head. "Are you wearing..."

"Yes," Kota said, and then blew a breath of air from his lips. "I'll explain later. She needs to hurry and get dressed."

Victor got out of the way to allow me to stand. Victor was a half a head taller than me. When I stood, he didn't hesitate to examine me again. I imagined that with bed hair and my groggy face, that I was pretty ugly.

Kota moved to the bathroom, opening the door and flicking the light on. "Does your bag have clean clothes?" he asked me.

I nodded to him.

"Get dressed and come down stairs when you're ready." He crossed the room and grabbed Victor by the arm. "Let's go."

"But..." Victor raked fingers through his hair, his fire eyes blazing with curiosity. When Kota yanked at his arm, he turned away. He looked back again when he was at the stairs going down, but said nothing more and soon disappeared.

I jumped for my book bag and ran for the bathroom. My heart pounded. Victor was just as handsome as Kota. He moved quickly to cover for me. How strange that a complete stranger, who knew less about me than Kota, was helping me.

People were not all murderers.

♥♥♥

I managed to do a quick job of washing my face and brushing my hair. I twisted my hair up, pulling it back into a clip at the back of my head, the locks of dirty blond hair falling from it tickling my neck. It was the way I always wore my hair, to keep it out of my face. I changed into a gray pleated skirt that was a little short, but was great for the warmer weather of the south. I had a soft button up blouse that matched it. I wanted to look nice to meet Kota's mom. I was lucky I had packed a couple of extra things into my bag besides shorts.

I felt sore and checked my hip. There was a dark purple bruise about the size of my palm at my side where I'd fallen. I'd have to remember to adjust my top and not show it. I didn't want Kota to feel bad again about what happened last night. Besides, it was pretty ugly. My shoes and clothes that I wore last night weren't in the tub where I left them. I was barefoot. How would I explain that?

I sighed and hurried downstairs. If I stayed too long, his mom would think I was weird.

At the base of the stairs, the rich aromas of fried eggs, bacon and buttered toast hit my nose. The dining room at the end of the hall had a small round table with five chairs near it; one was a mismatched office chair that Kota sat in. There was an empty space next to him and Victor on the other side. The other two chairs were occupied by a woman who looked to be in her late forties and a younger girl with glasses.

"Hello!" The older woman spotted me first and stood up, reaching out a hand. Her eyes were green like Kota's and her brown hair was tied into a bun at the back of her head. There were soft wrinkles at her eyes. She was almost my height. "It's nice to meet you. I'm Erica."

I smiled, blushing and reached to touch her hand delicately with my own.

I thought that would be it, but she took a firm grasp of my hand and gave it a good squeeze. "I haven't met your parents yet."

"We're still kind of settling in." She seemed so nice and I was scared she'd actually stop by my parents' house. I wanted to warn her that my mom probably wouldn't want to talk to her. There was only the hope that maybe she would forget.

"This is my daughter and Dakota's sister, Jessica." She pointed to the girl next to her. The girl was almost exactly like her mother, except shorter and with much lighter hair. Her expression was placid and she wore pink rimmed glasses. She nodded to me, almost shyly.

"Hi," I said. I blinked at the name Dakota and then realized she must have meant Kota. It struck me as funny, but I liked how he shortened it.

"Have a seat," Erica said. She motioned to the chair next to Kota and Victor.

The whole time we were talking, the guys fixed their eyes on me. Was my outfit bad? Maybe it was too much. I couldn't tell. The moment I sat down, Kota reached for the scrambled egg bowl and scooped a large spoonful on to my plate. Victor had the bacon platter and dropped a couple of slices next to the eggs.

"Orange juice?" Erica offered.

I smiled and nodded. I went to reach for it but Kota got to it first and held it above my cup.

"Say when."

I didn't notice that he had already started pouring. I quickly told him when it was enough and he recapped the bottle and put it back on the table.

I picked up my fork and knife, wondering if they were going to also cut my bacon into pieces. When I ate with my parents and my sister, it was pretty much a fend-for-yourself type of situation.

For a time, the table was quiet as everyone was eating, and it gave me a chance to notice some small things. Victor picked at his plate, eating the edge of his eggs and the chewy parts of his bacon. Kota cut his bacon into even pieces right from the start, with a formal poise that left me feeling uncivilized next to him. Jessica ate toast only. Erica was the only one who seemed to eat normally; her eyes were happy as she watched everyone at the table enjoying the meal.

"So how did you meet my son? And Victor?" Erica said. She had looked excitedly at the three of us the entire time, as if waiting for the right moment to ask this question.

I felt my mouth open slightly, my lips moved but the right answers didn't come to me.

"I met her yesterday," Kota said quickly.

"I only bumped into her today," Victor said, spearing a piece of bacon with his fork and the fire in his eyes lit up as he focused on me in an amused way. "Kind of surprised me, to be honest."

I blushed.

"Will you be going to their school?" Erica asked.

"Yup," Kota said. "She's in the same grade as us."

Erica's eyes flew from her son to Victor and back at me. "You've got such a lovely voice, Sang," she said, a small smile on her lips and lightly scolding tone. "And that ventriloquism thing you do is amazing. A real talent."

Kota and Victor both tinged red at the cheeks.

"You know how guys are," I said, offering a grin and a playful tone. "Give them two minutes, they think they know everything," I quipped.

Victor dropped his fork, gawking.

Kota laughed so hard his eyes shut and his hand went to his stomach.

25

Erica brightened. "Smart girl." She drummed her knuckles on the table and then stood, picking up her own dish. "Keep an eye on this one, Kota. She's got your number."

"Not yet, she doesn't," Kota said under his breath. His mother had turned away by then, but I heard it. He turned his face to me and winked. The reflection from the light caught in his glasses, giving him such a strange look, that I couldn't help but giggle.

When the rest of us finished, I attempted to help to clear the table, but Erica shooed us outside. "Don't waste the day. Go enjoy yourselves." She beamed a smile at me, looking so happy, I couldn't refuse.

Jessica headed off to another part of the house. Kota, Victor and I went outside. There was a hint of the chill left from the rain, but the sun was warming things up quickly. Small pools of water collected in spots in the yard. The concrete of the driveway was dry though and warmed my feet. I did like walking around barefoot outside but next to the guys who had on full socks and shoes, I felt like a bum.

Kota's dog was tethered to a lead at the back of the house. Now in the daylight, I laughed at seeing it was a Golden Retriever. Last night, it had felt like a horse. As soon as he saw us, he padded over, crossing the concrete drive to greet us. I ducked behind Kota, so he wouldn't jump on me again.

Kota spread out an arm, stopping Max with a palm held out in front of him. "No. Sit. You did enough damage already."

The dog obeyed, giving only the smallest of whines and then sinking down to a sitting position.

Victor looked at my bandaged hand. "So, that was from Max?"

I nodded. "It wasn't his fault. He just surprised me and I hit the pavement."

Victor looked sympathetic. Now thinking about the wound, my good hand moved to shield the bandages from the sun shining on it. It felt a little itchy. A gray BMW was parked in the driveway behind the brown sedan in the corner. I didn't know cars, but the BMW looked brand new.

"All right, out with it," Victor said. His arms crossed his chest and he looked firmly at the both of us. "I've been playing along all morning. I'd like to know what kind of trouble I'm digging myself into."

I glanced at Kota, but Kota gave no sign of hesitation. "She was out late walking home when Max broke the lead and... well... I couldn't just let her go home bleeding."

My heart fluttered, but I nodded, agreeing with him. "I was out so late that sneaking back in would have meant more trouble at my house."

"It just kind of happened," Kota followed up.

Victor looked back and forth at the two of us, as if trying to decide something. The fire in his eyes settled on me. The intensity was turned up so much, that it caused me to shiver and look away.

"Give her a break, Vic," Kota said. His body moved in front of me again, creating a block between the two of us. I looked around Kota's shoulder. Victor's eyes locked with mine. I wasn't sure what exchanged between us, but somehow Victor seemed to understand that whatever it was I wasn't telling him now, it was embarrassing, and maybe if we weren't complete strangers, I'd talk about it later.

"Okay," Victor said. He shrugged and then stuffed his hands into the pockets of his slacks. He nodded toward the BMW. "Well, I came over to take Kota to the mall. Are you going with us?"

Going out with them? To a mall? Could I get away with it? I wanted to go, but I also didn't want to intrude on plans already made. Would my parents send my sister to look for me and discover I wasn't around? No. Since we'd moved in, they hardly noticed when I left or came back. They got used to me walking around in the woods. I just needed to be careful. Still, as the guys looked at me and waited for an answer, I felt nervous about going out with them. Would they see me as the third wheel?

"Maybe we can put that off for a few hours," Kota said, I suppose sensing my hesitation.

"No." I shook my head, bending down to pet Max, who had been patiently sitting at Kota's feet. As soon as I started petting him, he rolled back to expose his belly for me to scratch. It also gave me a good deterrent to think of an excuse. "It's okay. You guys go. I've got things to do. I wouldn't want to slow you two down." I did want to go, though. I felt silly for wanting to, but I'd never had the opportunity before. Why did I have to be so shy and scared? I wished I could be normal.

Kota crouched next to me, his head turned toward my face. "Do you want to go?"

I shrugged, trying to look casual about it. "It probably doesn't matter. I wouldn't be allowed anyway." Crap. I hadn't meant to let that slip out.

Out of my peripheral vision, I could sense they were doing that thing again: exchanging looks. Their silent communication amazed me. I wanted to ask how long they knew each other, but just being around them, it felt like they were almost brothers.

"What if we went and asked?" Victor put his hands on his hips. "I mean, we're not ax murderers."

I couldn't help but smile at his words. His fire eyes sparked at what must have been a strange expression in that moment. "It's complicated. My mom would just say no right off. It won't matter who asks."

"We could try," Kota said.

I twisted my mouth, coming up with a plan. If I wasn't going to deter them from taking me with them, I wasn't about to let them into the lion's den to face off my parents. "If you really want me to go, give me a few minutes," I said.

"What are you going to do?" Kota asked, his head tilted and looking puzzled.

"She's going to lie, dummy," Victor said, the corner of his mouth moving down.

Kota frowned, standing up and rubbing at his chin. I noticed his nails were well manicured. "Really, it's no big deal if we go talk to them."

"I think it's better if I just make a quick appearance and then don't mention I'm going. They won't notice I'm missing for a few hours."

They shared another look and then Victor shrugged and turned back to me. "We'll wait."

I stood up and looked at both of them, edging away before turning to walk down the road. Would they really wait for me? Would I come back here and find them gone? I felt pathetic, wanting so bad to try to be cool so they would like me. I didn't know anyone and here were two guys... incredibly cute guys taking some sort of interest in someone like me. It felt unreal. I was average looking, I thought. I was a shy person. They didn't have a reason to be interested. They'd been so nice so far, though. I didn't want to ruin it yet.

"Wait," Kota said, coming up behind me. I turned and he was pointing to the house. "I forgot. Your shoes are inside."

I waved my hand in the air between us. "Oh yeah. And my bag."

He closed the space between us, bringing his face close to mine and whispering to me. "Is it okay for you to bring your bag home? Will they ask questions? Should I go get it?"

I smiled. Why did I feel so warmly fuzzy? Is this what having friends feels like? My expression must have been strange to read to Victor, who stood back at his car, leaning against it, his arms crossed over his chest. He looked puzzled, but kept his lips pursed.

"There's some back stairs at my house. As long as my sister doesn't take an interest, it should be okay."

He nodded and turned to Victor. "Just grabbing her stuff," he said. Kota crossed the drive to the garage and disappeared inside.

Victor's fire eyes smoldered at me, as I followed Kota

back into his house. My heart thumped against my breast the entire time. I had friends. Was it always this easy for people and I just never took the risk or had the opportunity? Anxiety threaded through me. How badly I wanted to not let this connection be severed. At the same time, it felt surreal. Maybe I was just imagining it and they were just being nice, but come tomorrow, they'd get bored and forget about me.

Would I ever feel comfortable being around other people?

♥♥♥

Five minutes later, I had dropped off my bag into my closet, grabbed a pair of sandals, and ran back outside. My dad was already at work. My mom was in her bedroom, and my sister was nowhere to be found.

No one in my family really gave me much notice unless they knew for sure I was with someone they didn't know. I was well known for exploring the woods and this neighborhood was surrounded by a wooded area that went on for quite a distance. The only warning my parents had told me when we first moved into the neighborhood was to not get lost and to not talk to anyone.

I had been right. Just leaving was better than asking. My only worry was someone might spot me getting into the car with the boys.

I exited the house through the side door that opened up to the large double-sided garage. Out in the driveway sat the BMW. I bit my lower lip and made a dash for the car.

Kota got out of the front passenger side. He held the door open for me, looking toward the house. "What did you say to them?"

"Nothing," I said quickly and hopped into the car, slipping into the smooth leather seat, feeling the coolness of the material on my thighs. The interior did smell brand new.

Kota looked over the top of the car, studying the house. In silence, I pleaded with him. *Just get in and let's go*, I thought. *It'll be fine unless someone spots us.* I knew they really couldn't understand why I needed to sneak out. If they tried to ask my parents or forced the issue, this friendship between us would be over before it ever got a chance.

His eyes swept over the two-story gray home. There was a wide concrete porch out front, a two-car garage on the outside, a screened-in porch in the back, and a separate shed toward the end of the driveway. The yard was at least an acre. It was a little bigger than the rest of the homes in the neighborhood, but not overly so. I wondered what he thought of a girl who would live in such a place and yet dashed off in the middle of the night. I assumed he probably thought I was a complete brat, unhappy with not getting my own way. I wanted to tell him how untrue that was. The house was big, but it was hollow. A prison that my mother felt was protection, but kept me from being a normal teenager for years.

He turned away from the house at last and climbed into the back seat. The breath I'd been holding escaped from between my lips. In the back of my mind, I knew someday I'd have to explain my family to Kota if I wanted to remain friends with him. He was smart and would catch on. Would he tell Victor or other kids at school how strange I was? Would they refuse to have anything to do with me if they knew the truth?

Victor put the car into reverse. My eyes locked directly on the house, and I could only hope I wouldn't be spotted. I couldn't explain to my parents what this was. There was no way to prove to my mother that Kota and Victor weren't going to rape me or force heroin into my system. Of course, I didn't have proof, but I'd always known most people weren't really like that. Not everyone in the world was evil, like my mother told me nearly every day for over fifteen years. No matter what, my family could never know about Kota and Victor. When I had time to get the boys to like me better, I'd try to explain it to them.

Was it silly wanting someone to like me so much as

much as I wanted Kota and Victor to like me? It was the first time I ever had friends. It felt so important now, something that last night wasn't even on my mind.

No matter what, I had to keep this separation, putting up a wall between my family life and my private life outside of the house.

$\mathscr{S}$ILAS

$\mathscr{V}$ictor drove the half circle that was Sunnyvale Court and was out on the highway within a few minutes. He met up with the interstate a couple miles away, heading east into Charleston. I had no idea where this mall was. Two rules broken. I was with strangers and I was lost.

In my excitement, I hadn't paid attention to the conversation between Victor and Kota.

"Is he answering?" Victor said, adjusting the rear view mirror as he sped down the road.

"Hey, you ready?" Kota asked. I turned to see he had pulled out a cell phone; one palm was against his ear and the other pressing the phone to his head. "We're almost there."

"Who are we getting?" I asked Victor.

"An ax murderer." He grinned, the fire in his eyes lighting up. He glanced over at me. "Will you please buckle in? It's bad enough we kidnapped you."

I hid my smile from him, rather liking the idea that these cute guys kidnapped me. That meant they wanted me around, right? My heart was racing at this adventure. Not wanting to get too carried away, I reached for the seat belt and strapped myself in.

Victor started playing with the radio, scanning through stations.

"That's good," Kota said at a rock station. Victor ignored him and skipped to another one. "That one's fine, too." I didn't know if Kota was interested in the music or more worried that Victor wasn't really paying attention to his driving. He seemed nervous.

Victor frowned, flipping away from the station. Soon he landed on one that was playing an orchestral piece. He stopped and turned up the volume, the violin tempo rapid. "Will this put you to sleep?" Victor asked me.

"I love Vivaldi."

His mouth popped open, his hand temporarily letting go of the steering wheel. "What did you say?"

My eyes went wide and I nodded to the wheel. He recovered and took it over again. "I said I like Vivaldi. Summer is okay," I said, motioning to the radio that was playing the piece. "I like Winter best though."

Victor's lips pursed but his eyes held that same fire. He glanced up at the mirror and I knew he was sharing another look with Kota. I was trying to figure out this secret language they shared. Did he think I was weird because I knew some classical music or even admitted that I liked it? Maybe this was a test. Would I ever be able to understand?

We pulled off the interstate and took a short drive into an apartment complex. I was leaning against the window, feeling the sun on my face. There was an empty swimming pool near the front and tennis courts and a large pond in the middle with two fountains. The whole place looked more like a resort.

"Will you stop being cute? Your nose is smudging the window. My god, you're worse than a puppy," Victor said, making a slow turn through the complex.

I blushed and sat back. Victor glanced back at me, a playful smirk on his face. His request had me wondering if he was displeased but he didn't appear to be. "Sorry," I said.

"She's new," Kota said. "She's going to be interested in stuff."

"I got that, Sherlock, thank you," Victor said, tilting his head slightly as he talked to his friend, glancing at him in the mirror. He pulled up to a row of cars at the last building of the complex and then yanked the stick to park his car. "Let's go get Silas."

"Who's Silas?" I asked, unbuckling, feeling goofy since I just put the thing on. I wasn't even sure if he had been talking to me, but I didn't want to wait in the car. My skin was tingling with being free. With friends. Out in their car. It was hard not to be so excited.

"Goes to our school," Kota said after he got out. He pointed toward the last door on the second floor. "Head on up."

When we got to the second floor, Victor tugged me by the arm. "Stand here," he said, pointing to the spot just in front of Silas's door. I moved where he told me to. He buzzed the doorbell and stepped back, pulling Kota with him against the wall.

I just realized he was leaving me to face Silas alone, when the door opened. The guy was at least a head and a half taller than Kota. His hair was a deep black, shining with a light behind him reflecting on it. His eyes were a deep brown, almost black in the shadow of the overhang over the apartment. His jaw was firm, squared. His muscles under his black Red Sox t-shirt were prominent. Even his dark blue Levis looked bulky at the thighs. He was raw power.

I was speechless. I wasn't sure what to say or how to respond. Silas stared down at me, looking confused.

"Do you have the wrong place?" he asked. His voice was deep, nearly reverberating through me.

"What a pick up line," Victor piped in.

Silas twisted where he stood to see Victor leaning against the wall, his arms folded at his chest. Kota stood behind him, looking as if he wasn't sure if he should be laughing and had the palm of his hand up against the back of his head, half shrugging.

"Who's she?" Silas demanded.

"I'm Sang," I said.

Silas turned to me and raised a thick dark eyebrow. "Huh?" The way he peered down at me, I knew it wasn't his fault, but he made me feel so small. "Say that again." I picked up that he had an accent. It was very slight. I want to say European. His thick lips curled in a way when he talked that had me wanting to ask him to say more things, too.

"My name is Sang," I said.

"She moved into a house down the road from mine," Kota explained. "She's coming along."

Silas's forehead wrinkled and he blew out an impatient huff, but shrugged and waved me off. "Let me close the door." As he stood in front of his door, I could see how broad his shoulders were. There was a slight gruff look to his face, as if he didn't shave that morning. It made him look a lot more handsome, but it also made him look older. Since he was so tall, too, it was hard to imagine we were in the same grade.

"We've got to work on your people skills," Victor said as we headed back to his car. "You're supposed to at least say hello when you answer the door."

"She looked lost," Silas said. I kept taking peeks at his face. His features were striking. Soulful deep eyes and an olive complexion. He looked over at me and I blushed at getting caught staring. "I didn't scare you, did I?" he asked.

I shook my head, although a little too quickly. I wanted to say something convincing, but the truth was he did kind of scare me. I didn't want to admit it, but being in a dark alley with him and not knowing who he was would have probably been enough to make me pee my pants.

He only looked partially relieved, and I wasn't quite sure if he believed me.

Back at the car, Kota opened the passenger door, looking intently at me, waiting for me to get in.

"Silas should take the front seat," I said. "He's got longer legs."

"I don't mind," Silas said.

"Neither do I." I didn't mean to be so persistent, but if I was going to get them to like me, I had to do nice things. I didn't need to be coddled because I was the girl. Also, I had no idea how far away this mall was. What if he was bottled up for an hour?

He tilted his head from side to side, as if weighing out the situation. Something softened in his face.

"Someone get in," Victor called. He was already behind the wheel.

Kota moved away from the door and when I didn't budge, Silas got into the front seat. I was actually relieved. I would have felt terrible to see Silas have to get behind me and have to scrunch his knees.

I sat next to Kota, this time remembering to plug in my seat belt. Kota did the same and we were off.

Silas immediately reached for the radio to fiddle with it, but Victor slapped at his hand. "Hey, when you drive, you get to pick."

"Sang wouldn't like this stuff," he said.

"She already said she did."

Silas raised an eyebrow and turned to me. "Is he shitting me?"

I raised my fingers to my mouth, the tips playing with my lower lip. "I, uh..."

"She likes it," Kota said for me.

"But I like rock, too," I said quickly. "And some other stuff. I like a lot of different types of music."

Silas shot Victor a cocky smile. "You're outnumbered. Kota likes rock."

"Kota likes anything."

I gave a sideways glance to Kota. He slipped a conspiratorial grin and I smiled back, silently amused at the conversation.

The two continued to argue about the radio, switching between stations at every other song. Victor groaned about squeaky guitars and Silas complained about being put to sleep by a piano. They were all so different. How in the world did they become friends?

I was watching out the window at the trees and cars that we passed, trying to remember the direction Victor was taking. The palm trees were the most striking to me. Having lived up north for so long, it was strange to me. Everything was green and the sky appeared to be a slightly different shade of blue, lighter, crisp and full of promise.

Soon the interstate had signs promising a mall and the

car was pulling into the lot of a shopping center that looked bigger than any of the handful I'd ever seen.

As soon as the car was parked, Silas jumped out and opened my door for me. I blushed, thanked him, and stepped away so he could shut it.

We walked in through the closest department store together. Kota held open the first set of doors for all of us, Silas held open the second set. I smiled to myself about it. I wondered if it was normal, or if they were trying to be nice, since I was new.

The mall wasn't too crowded. The boys took only a moment to get oriented and then set off in a direction, walking past stores. They started talking and I fell behind them, unsure what to say, unsure who to walk with. I hadn't even noticed I had done it. It just seemed like the natural thing to do. Bits of the conversation drifted to me, but they were moving quickly, I was just trying to make sure I was keeping up.

I was peeking in at stores, checking out what was open, when Victor stopped short in front of me and I crashed into him. My chest hit his back, my hands met his hips, and my lips brushed at the back of his neck at the base, a little too hard as my lip tingled after. My breath caught and I backed off of him quickly, embarrassed.

Victor's face tinged red as he looked back at me. "Christ, you scared me. I was just wondering where you'd gone." His hand went to the back of his neck and then his head tilted, his mouth opening in surprise. I supposed he realized what must have happened. I practically accidentally kissed his neck.

"Sorry. I didn't mean to be following you so closely."

"You shouldn't be walking behind us," Kota said.

"Yeah. Come on. Walk up here with us," Silas offered. He reached out, taking my hurt wrist, only I winced. He noticed and he pulled me close, turning my hand over and checking out the bandages. "Who did this to you?" His eyes widened at me, intent and almost harsh, expecting an answer.

"It was Max," Kota said. "He jumped on her and she

didn't expect it."

How many times would we have to tell this story?

Silas seemed satisfied. "I'm sorry if I hurt you."

I shook my head. "I'm fine." My voice was softer than I meant for it to be, but his show of concern had my heart pounding fast. I wanted to press a palm to my chest at the whirl of emotions I was feeling around them. Meeting one nice person like Kota was fine. Three in twenty-four hours? It amazed me again at how wrong my parents were about the outside world.

Silas took my arm again, gentler this time, and guided me until I was walking next to him. Victor and Kota stood at his other side. Again we started to walk, and this time they moved slower so I could keep up.

"Where are we going?" I asked. They seemed to pass by a lot of interesting shops without looking at any of them.

"We're going to get fitted for some new suits," Victor said.

I glanced at Silas and Kota. "All of you?"

They nodded, looking as if this was as expected.

"Are these school clothes?" I scratched absentmindedly at my wrist. It hadn't occurred to me that the new school, even if it was a public one, might require uniforms or something. Would I need to wear something specific?

The three exchanged glances. Silas slipped his hands into his pockets. Victor cleared his throat but said nothing. Kota spoke up. "Sort of. Just for the nicer events. We thought it'd be easier to get it done now instead of when all those formal dances start happening."

Was that normal? How strange. I would have never thought of that.

We came up to a men's clothing store and at the entryway, the three guys were greeted by a male attendant. Kota approached him quickly, leaning his head into him to talk.

Silas stepped up to me, cutting off my view of Kota. His hands were in his pockets and he looked down at me. "Did you want to go look around somewhere else?"

Was he trying to get rid of me? I wasn't sure, but before I could answer, Victor piped in.

"Have her stay," he said. Silas turned to him but Victor looked at me. "There's usually a couch or something around here."

"I don't want her to get bored," Silas said.

"She won't be bored." Victor came closer to me, a gleam amid the fire in his eyes. "Do you have a phone on you?"

I shook my head, blushing at revealing how out of touch I was. Who our age didn't have a cell phone?

He reached into his back pocket. "See, Silas? If she walked off, we would have had to hunt her down. I don't want to lose her." Victor passed me what looked like the latest iPhone. "Play some Angry Birds. Download whatever app you want. We won't be long."

Kota and the attendant waited for Silas and Victor to join them. Silas passed me a look, not seeming too displeased that I was actually sticking around.

I held Victor's phone to my chest, still feeling the warmth of his body that had heated up the metal cover. I found a small sofa not far from the entrance and sat down. The leather of the seat was cool against my bare legs but also sticky. I folded my skirt down, smoothing out the material and then rechecked to make sure the shirt was fully covering the bruise on my back. The boys disappeared into the back of the store.

I was too nervous to even look at Victor's phone at first. What sort of things could I learn about him? How trusting was he that he simply handed his phone to me without a flinch of concern? I swore to myself I wouldn't betray his trust.

A couple of attendants materialized next to me and asked politely if there was something they could do for me. I declined each time, expressing that I was only waiting. As other customers started poking through racks of clothes nearby, I appeared to be really interested in the phone. I found the Angry Birds app and became engrossed with knocking over pigs.

"Sang. What do you think?"

I looked up and my breath simply disappeared from my lungs. I felt my jaw drop and the phone almost slipped from my hands. Kota appeared in front of me in a black suit with light charcoal pinstripes. I caught sight of a tag against the sleeve that said Armani. Wasn't that really expensive? He wore a black collared dress shirt underneath. The whole ensemble was fitted to frame his body, and it showed. The cut was very nice. "What do you think of the black shirt?" His finger caught the bridge of his glasses and he slid them a little higher on his nose. He turned to show me the side, smoothing out the material of the jacket.

My heart was doing flip flops. He could have modeled for the catalog. He was asking my opinion? I leaned forward, feeling the words rushing from my mouth. "It's gorgeous." It was the most awkward thing to say and I regretted it the moment it slipped from my lips.

He blushed, but I caught the corner of his mouth drifting up. "I mean do you think it'd be better in white? You know, something more traditional?"

I shook my head. "It'd detract from the stripes. Though you'd probably want a tie. Maybe in red?" I had never been asked my opinion on fashion. I had a fledgling idea of what looked good to me. When it came to my own clothes, I just tried to match what I saw on television and what the other students were wearing.

He seemed to consider what I was saying. "Elegant," he said softly. He smiled at me, seeming satisfied with my answer. "You're not too bored, are you?"

I lifted the phone in my hand to half show it to him. "Level fifteen of Angry Birds."

He beamed. "We're just wrapping up." He waved to me and disappeared back among the racks of jackets and pants.

I was on level twenty when the guys came back. They were empty-handed. For some reason I had thought they would bring back those clothes in bags, but then I remembered this was a fitting. The attendants probably needed to make some alterations.

"Hey, you," Victor said when he spotted me. His hands were in his pockets and his cheeks were flushed. His expression confused me and I stood up quickly to greet them. I handed his phone back. He took it from me, checking the screen. "You're quick. And all three stars."

My smile faltered a little. "I didn't ruin your game, did I?"

He looked up quickly. "No," he said and he tucked his phone back into his pocket.

"He's just twitterpated," Silas said. The shadow of a grin stretched from his face, as if he'd just been laughing and was about to start into another fit.

Victor shot out a fist to punch at Silas's arm. "Shut up or I'm leaving you here."

I looked to Kota. He shook his head and rolled his eyes. "Come on. Let's do something else."

"Where do you want to go, Sang?" Silas asked.

I thought about it. "Is it bad if I say can we just walk around? I'd like to see what's here."

"A sensible request," Kota said.

We left the store. Again I was next to Silas at the end with Victor and Kota on the other side of him. This time, instead of talking to each other, they took the time to point out different shops they thought I'd be interested in -- mostly clothing and shoes. I hid my grin at their attempts to catch my eye and see if I was impressed. I wasn't sure what they wanted me to say.

We were circling an atrium where the mall split into different directions, when someone walking by bumped hard into me. I staggered backward, catching myself before I fell. My hand went back to my arm, protective of the wound.

"Hey!" Silas spun around. He caught me by the shoulders and brought me close to him before turning his head at the guy that had bumped into me. "Watch where you're going." His voice was deeper now, almost a growl.

My heart thundered in my chest. Silas's hands felt so big as he held on to my shoulders, and he stood so close that I felt his body warmth. I think it made me more nervous than the confrontation.

"Dude, she bumped into me." The guy had dark hair, was thin, had a goatee and looked about our age. He had a couple of friends lingering behind him. Their pants hung low on their hips and they all wore oversized sport t-shirts. The guy who'd bumped into me gave me a look, tilted his head back and directed his chin at me. "Hey girl."

"I saw you lean into her," barked Silas. He moved in front of me, shielding me. I gasped a little, stuttering. I wanted to say let's get going, but I couldn't mouth the words. He seemed so angry. He turned his head back toward me. "Just stay behind me," he said.

"Dude, fuck you. You don't know shit." The guy was slurring his words a little, making it difficult to understand him.

"Come on, Silas," Kota said. I glanced at Victor. His fists were clenched, his jaw was set as he glared at the guys, but he didn't move. It was like he was waiting for something. I shot him a look and he caught my eyes. I gave a quick shake, my eyes wide, silently pleading with him just to back off. *Let's go,* I urged wordlessly. *I don't want trouble.*

There was a silence that lingered on; my hands started to tremble. I reached up to Silas to touch his back, warming my palm against him.

Suddenly Silas turned around and urged me forward. Kota and Victor followed. This time Silas put me on the other side, so I was walking between him and Victor.

"Should I..." I started to say.

"Just keep moving," Silas ordered through clenched teeth.

We turned into another part of the mall and passed a few stores before Silas pointed at a bookstore and we moved together into it. Victor grasped my good wrist, guiding me to the back. My heart was about to explode. It was close enough that he was almost holding my hand.

Silas and Kota stayed near the front, glancing at the new novels on racks near the wide windows. They occasionally glanced at the door.

At the back near the children's books, Victor tugged me out of the aisle and pushed me until my back was against a wall of books, hiding me from view from the front. He checked around me, glancing toward the door. He pulled back to face me. His fire eyes held a glaze as he looked at me and he brushed back a lock of hair that had fallen into my eyes. "You okay?"

I nodded and tried to speak but hadn't realized my throat was dry. I swallowed and then started again. "It's fine. Did they walk away?"

"I think they followed us a little but lost interest. Just hanging out for a moment to make sure."

I wasn't sure how to suggest it, but it was almost like it was rehearsed, the way they worked together. Without talking, they split up and knew exactly how to handle things. There was nothing for me to say. It wasn't like it was possible or that they planned the situation. Like their silent communication, I supposed, was it just something they managed to do together? Do good friends get to know each other so well, it's like they can simply work in a coordinated fashion?

Kota poked his head around the bookshelf. It spooked me a little, but I caught myself. "You guys okay?"

I nodded, smiling.

"We're good," Victor said.

"We'll just hang around a few more minutes. Just look like you're browsing."

"No problem," I said. Now that the situation felt over, I was glancing at book titles, my eyes instantly attracted to some of the thicker volumes.

"You like books?" Victor asked, catching my look.

"Who doesn't?"

Kota almost gave a hoot in laughter. I didn't catch what was so funny. Victor just smiled. "Have at it," he said, ushering with a hand for me to lead the way.

I felt like they were going to follow me. I hadn't anticipated that. I lost myself in the shelves, checking for the fiction section and then noting the authors and cover styles of the novels.

"I think it's grouped by genre," Kota said.

I knelt, looking at a few titles I recognized. "It's kind of mixed up. I think these are more horror but they've lumped them with general fiction."

He looked over my head to check out what I was pointing to. He put his hand on my shoulder. It seemed such a casual touch, again something I'd seen other people do or read about. He seemed to do it without thinking and yet my mind was filled for the moment with nothing but the warmth of his fingers. He was so close that I could smell the sweet spice of his cologne. I felt my body tingling. It felt so intimate to me. "Do you like horror?" he asked.

"Not spooky. More psychologically scary. Something a little bit smarter than a guy with a knife hiding behind a wall."

"You like smart killers?"

"I like figuring out the best way to handle bad situations," I said, although after the words slipped from my mouth, I realized it sounded weird.

When I looked back at him, a grin slipped away from his face. "What else do you like?"

Victor had disappeared. Being alone with Kota now made my stomach twist, especially since he insisted on standing so close. I couldn't back away unless I wanted to bump into the bookshelves. Was it normal for friends to stand so close to each other? I wished he'd stop looking at my eyes and face. I wanted to shield myself from it. "Depends on my mood, I guess. Mystery, fantasy..."

His head tilted. "Classics?"

"British, preferably. Sherlock Holmes or King Arthur. Although I did like Gone with the Wind."

Silas appeared from behind Kota. His brows were creased and he had his arms tucked into his body, as if trying not to touch anything. "I'm pretty sure they're gone."

"Good," Kota said, straightening up and giving me enough room to stand next to him now. "The last thing we need right now is an altercation."

Silas nodded in agreement, but glanced at me and then dodged his head around, his eyes scanning the store. "Where'd Vic go?"

"We'll get him," Kota said. That gentle power from Kota's voice became more prominent. Why did it feel like he was giving orders? "Meet you in the front."

Silas nodded and headed back.

"He doesn't care for bookstores," Kota explained to me as we wound our way to the end of the aisle. "The lanes are narrow and he hates bumping into them."

I smiled to myself at the thought of Silas being so concerned, but I couldn't imagine him clumsy. He seemed to be fully in control of his body.

It turned out we didn't need to hunt for Victor. He was up front making a purchase. The store attendant was just putting it into a plastic bag as we approached.

"What'd you get?" I asked.

He turned to me, smiling coolly. "Some sheet music."

"He plays piano," Kota explained.

Victor narrowed his eyes at him. "I was going to tell her."

Kota bowed his head, looking apologetic. "Sorry."

"It's okay," I said, trying to lighten the mood. "I'm jealous. It'd be really neat to learn to play."

"Why haven't you?" Kota asked.

I shrugged. "Never had a piano to fiddle with." My father made enough money for a big house, but he always said he couldn't afford to keep up with the whims of his kids; he rarely allowed things that cost money. I wanted to try to explain it, but it felt too awkward, too soon.

Again, looks were exchanged between Kota and Victor. That was going to drive me crazy. I vowed to myself to try to catch their looks and understand this language they had between them. Were they feeling sorry for me? Confused? Did they think I was pathetic? Were they going to laugh about the poor stupid girl later whose parents wouldn't buy her a piano and walked alone in the rain at night?

We left the bookstore and continued the tour. Walking between Silas and Victor was awkward. I was either brushing arms with one or the other and I kept trying to make my shoulders sink in, drawing my arms into my body. I was walking like an idiot, doing my best to not touch them. I wasn't supposed to get so close so soon that I could just walk with my arm touching someone else's, was I? Since I wasn't sure what was appropriate, the best thing to do seemed to be to keep a distance.

After a while, my shoulders were sore. It wasn't necessary anyway; no matter how I walked, Silas eventually needed to lean into me to get out of the way of people walking by and Victor walked like a snake, swaying back and forth across his path. As soon as I relaxed, Silas's forearm brushed against mine. I was sure people thought we were holding hands. Victor, on occasion, bumped into me, and smiled when it happened. Something told me he was doing it on purpose.

I could smell the food court before we ever saw it. Silas's hand went right to his abs. His stomach gurgled. I glanced up at him, trying not to laugh at his mortified expression. He gave me a half smile and nodded. "I think it's time for some lunch."

"How about sushi?" Victor suggested. "Do you like fish, Sang?"

"No fish," Kota interjected before I could answer. "Not after last time."

"I wasn't going to take her there," he said.

Silas shot him a look.

Victor gave a frustrated sigh. "Sang, what do you want?"

"I didn't bring any money, guys," I said, blushing. I didn't want to add that I didn't have any at all to bring. My father didn't give allowances. "You all pick something you like. I'm still kind of full from breakfast anyway." That wasn't really true. I was actually kind of hungry now that I was smelling frying oil and sweets.

"You're getting something," Silas commanded.

"Besides, Victor's paying."

My mouth popped open in an 'o' expression.

Victor nodded with confidence. "It's my turn, anyway."

It was a thing, I thought. They took turns buying each other lunch? I wondered when my turn would be. It would be really embarrassing when they discovered I couldn't repay them like this.

There was a small debate about where to eat, but Kota suggested a hamburger place. Victor got an Angus beef hamburger with Swiss and mushrooms, holding the condiments. Silas ordered three double cheeseburgers and a large fry. I mimicked Kota's order, a chicken sandwich and medium fries.

Victor removed a black credit card from his wallet and swiped it. His parents gave him a credit card? From what I'd read about in books, black credit cards were reserved for the really rich. Maybe the novels I'd read weren't accurate, so I dismissed it. After the order was paid for, I whispered a quick thank you to him. He blinked at me, his face turning red, but he waved me off.

Silas shooed us away to find a spot to sit while he waited on the order. We filled our drinks and then walked out into the middle of the sea of tables and chairs that surrounded a running carousel. I wanted to point to a spot close to the middle to see the paint on the horses, but Kota was the first one to suggest a spot, one close to the outer edge of the courtyard. The food court wasn't crowded, but he picked the place furthest away from where other people were sitting.

We got to the table and Victor quickly pulled a chair out, looking directly at me. I blinked, muttered a thank you, and allowed him to slide the chair in behind me as I sat. Victor sat next to me, across from Kota. Silas plopped down in front of me with the tray of food.

"People are animals when they get hungry," Silas said. "The guy behind me was demanding a taco."

I laughed and Silas's dark eyes lit up. He passed the food around.

Silence fell over the table as we ate. I finished my

sandwich and was nibbling on my fries as the guys finished up and started talking again. I was half paying attention to what they were talking about. I focused on people who appeared to be friends. I watched how they walked together. Sometimes they touched. Sometimes they had hands stuffed into their pockets and they bumped the other one in the direction they wanted to go without talking.

Normal. This is normal. My mind whirled, worrying this day would end too soon. Who knows when I would get another chance to just hang out like this? Would they even care to invite me again? It probably didn't matter. After today, they'd get over being nice to the new girl. Either that, or my mom would find out the truth, eventually. I shoved those thoughts to the back of my mind. I was being paranoid and it annoyed me. I was being as self-destructive as my own mother, thinking like that.

Motion across the walkway caught my attention. The guy with the goatee and his friends were leaning against the wall of a video game store. The guy with the goatee folded his arms over his chest and he made kissing faces my way. At first my eyes widened but I tried to adjust myself, attempting to look bored and disinterested. He laughed, but I slowly turned my eyes as if I hadn't even noticed. I wasn't sure if I was able to hide the blush I felt in my cheeks. I pulled myself back into the conversation, forcing myself to nibble at another fry, even though I was full.

"You can't be serious," Victor was saying to Kota. "Not another physics class. You've already taken all of them."

"Not a particle physics one."

"Tell me they don't even offer that class," Victor rubbed a palm at his eye, looking pained. "It's so pointless. It's theoretical. You won't use it."

Silas shook his head. He caught me looking at him and offered a grin. I shared one back, pointing the open end of my fries at him.

"You don't want any more?"

"I'm stuffed," I said.

He reached for the carton, his fingers brushing mine. A

spark started from my fingertips and then ignited in my belly. His fingers were a little coarse, but strong and warm.

"Thanks," he said. His voice was softer now. Had he felt the same thing I did? "What classes are you going to take?" he asked.

I gave a small glance to Kota, who was so engrossed in trying to explain his desired classes, that he hadn't heard Silas. Was I now used to Kota answering for me? "There are a few prerequisites, aren't there? I was going to fill up on those."

"You should take something you like," Silas said. "It can't be all work. Unless you're like Kota." He jerked his head in Kota's direction and then stuffed his mouth with some fries.

I laughed, shrugging a little. "I don't really know yet. I only glanced at the catalog; some of the more interesting things, I can't take yet."

"Like what..."

"Oh my god," Victor said, his voice rising. The fire burned, his eyes narrowing. "Okay, I'm done. Sang, are you finished? I can't talk to him."

Kota looked perplexed. "You were asking..."

"I'm not asking anymore!" Victor raised his hands in the air, waving in defeat. "You win. We're good. Let's just do something else."

I shared another grin with Silas, even though I wasn't totally sure I understood what was going on.

"I'm headed to the bathroom real quick. I'll be right back." Victor stood, pushing his chair away. He grabbed his bag and started to walk off. He'd left his trash on the table.

Kota collected his own wrappers and Victor's and put it all on the tray. "I'll be right back. Maybe I should go apologize." He walked off after Victor.

"Good luck," Silas said. He stood up, grabbing the tray and took my empty wrapper to add to it. "I'll get rid of this. Wait here."

I smiled, shaking my head. The boys were interesting. Silas looked around for a place to throw the trash. He walked around groups of people waiting in line for their kids at the carousel. He disappeared behind the swirling horses.

"Hey, princess," a voice behind me said. I turned around. The guy with the goatee sat in Silas's seat. His oversized red shirt billowed around his lean frame. His lips curled like he was constantly kissing the air. "Your boys left you?"

His pungent cologne mixed with menthol cigarette smoke drifted from across the table making my nose wrinkle. "They'll be right back," I said.

He nodded with a sharp tilt. The way he did it made his chin angular and thin. "What's your name, sweetie?"

I just looked at him, not sure what to say. His friends were still across the hallway, watching the two of us. Why did he care? Why did I get the feeling I shouldn't talk to him? I mean, I knew he bumped into me but should I judge a person for being careless?

"I said, what's your name?" he asked again.

"I'm Sang."

"Sang? That's just fucking weird. Do you sing?"

I shook my head, blushing. My heart was pounding, but not in the same way it had been with Silas and the others. This was different. The bad feeling inside of me had my mind whirling, echoing the negativity my mother whispered to me about what happened to girls when they went out.

"I'm Greg." He patted a hand on his chest, and tilted his chin toward me. "We should go out. What's your number?"

"I'm sorry. I should go." I stood up, pushing my chair in. My hand flew up to my chest, rubbing over my thudding heart. Silas was still missing. Where did they go?

Greg stood and followed me. I sought out the restrooms. If the guys weren't around, I was going to dart into the girl's bathroom where he couldn't follow.

I broke away from him and walked around tables, heading toward the opening to the hallway where there were signs for restrooms. As I got to the hallway, Greg continued on my heels. "Hey, I was asking you out. Why are you walking off like that?"

"I'm already out," I said, my hands turning into fists reflexively, feeling cornered.

"Who did that to your hand?" he said, pointing at my bandages. He leapt forward and closed the distance between us. "Those guys hurt you?" His voice was grating, varying in pitch and then there was the sharp way he ended his questions. Compared to Kota's powerful, Victor's smooth baritone and Silas's deep voice, Greg's made me shiver cold.

I stepped away from him, forcing some distance between us. I met with a wall, smacking up against it. I gasped, trying to slip to the side to get out of his way. My heart was racing, feeling trapped.

Greg drew closer, putting his forearm over my head against the wall above me and looking down at me. He wasn't that much taller than me, maybe only a couple of inches. "You shouldn't let those guys do things like that to you. Unless you like pain? Is that your kink?"

My mouth dropped open. "Seriously, I'm not interested. I'm sorry."

His mouth went up a fraction at the corner, smirking. "Is it because you're dating one of those guys? Which one?"

I shook my head, not sure how to answer.

"It's the tall one, isn't it? I could tell. You fuck him yet?"

My mouth was dry and I choked out a no to respond. Why did I think I could get back here and escape him? Where was Kota?

He laughed and leaned in to me. "Come on. How about this? Kiss me, and I'll leave you alone. I bet you'll leave that guy and walk out of here with me." His mouth was close to mine and I nearly gagged as I could taste the stale menthol on his breath. My heart raced and I had my head backed up. I wanted to push him away, but I didn't want to touch him.

"Why are you moving away?" he demanded. His fingers wrapped around my chin, holding my face still. His fingers dug into my cheeks and I gasped because it hurt. His eyes fixed on my mouth and he lowered his head.

A hand landed on Greg's shoulder, yanking him back.

Greg flew into the air. He toppled, falling. His body hit the far wall and he slid down until he was sitting on the floor, looking dazed.

Kota stepped between us, his hands positioned in a stance I'd seen in karate movies. *Holy crap, Kota knows Kung Fu.*

My mouth opened to say something but I couldn't form the words. Victor materialized next to me. He took one look at Greg and then grabbed for my good hand. He wrapped his fingers around my palm and pulled me out of the hallway without a word. Kota remained behind. Would he get hurt when Greg recovered? Could Kota defend himself?

Victor pulled me back out into the food court and we weaved our way around tables. My mind was everywhere: Greg's bad breath lingering in my nose, the image of Kota flipping him over, Victor's palm pressing into mine.

Silas was leaning against our table. He took one look at Victor's face and he stood up. "Where's Kota?"

"In the hallway. He's got it. We're leaving."

Silas's eyes scanned the food court for the hallway. "I'm going to check. We'll meet you at the car."

Victor held on to me as we nearly jogged out of the mall. His thumb brushed at the crevice between my thumb and forefinger. My palm started to sweat and I was embarrassed about it, but he didn't seem fazed. The silence between us left room to worry about Kota and Silas, and I wished we could go back and check on them.

Victor didn't let go of me until we got to his car, so he could take his keys out. Victor handed off his plastic bag to me as he unlocked the car.

"Get in behind me," he said. "I'm going to pull up to the curb so they can get in quickly."

What if they got hurt? I hadn't seen Greg's friends around, but they must have noticed he went in there and Silas going in after them. I held the plastic bag up to my chest, folding my arms over it and trying to breathe slowly. This was my fault. I should have stuck with Silas.

Victor started the car and made a loop around the

parking lot until he pulled up next to the curb in front of the department store doors. We waited. My breath caught every time the doors opened and it wasn't the guys.

"Come on..." Victor urged under his breath, his hands twisting at the wheel.

Two minutes later, Silas and Kota both appeared at the doors and stepped out. They tried to look casual but they were walking double time and went right for the car. Silas climbed in back with me and Kota took the front seat.

I kept my eyes glued to the door of the mall as Victor pulled away. I turned, putting my knees in the seat and facing backwards to look out the rear window to watch for any sign of Greg or his friends.

"Are they out there?" Victor asked.

"I don't see them," I said.

"I think we lost them," Kota said, sounding breathless, leaning against the seat. "Only I got worried when we made a circle in one department store trying to shake them."

"Sang, it's all right. You can sit," Silas said. His finger jabbed me in my side. Unfortunately, it was the side that was bruised and, not expecting it, I winced and cried out an "*Ouch,*" before I could catch myself.

Silas's eyes widened. His large hand pushed me back up against the seat, holding me there. He lifted my blouse away from the top of my skirt. I could feel cool air on the bruise and I shivered.

"Where did that come from?" he demanded.

"I..."

He let go of me, turning his body to face the door. His hand clutched the handle. "Turn the car around."

"Silas," Kota started.

His fists clenched and he spoke through his teeth. "I said turn it around."

"It wasn't him," I said quickly. I felt eyes fall on me again. I swallowed, feeling my stomach twisting. "That's from yesterday. Greg never touched me."

The car fell into silence. I turned around, sliding into place and sitting back.

"Was it from Max?" Kota asked in a quiet tone.

I averted my eyes, focusing on the back of Victor's seat. "Yes," I said quietly. My lip quivered and I bit at it to stop it. How to ruin a friendship in less than a day? Lie about your injuries and get the guys into trouble over some stranger. I felt the anxiety clutching my chest. This was it. They're going to get rid of me the first chance they got.

"Let me see it again," Kota said. The power disappeared from his voice, replaced with something assuring, gentle. "Sang, let me see."

I got up like I had been before. Silas assisted me with raising my shirt up a little. He tucked two fingers into the top hem of my skirt and pulled it down an inch to reveal the splotch of purple.

Kota made a face. "Sang, I'm so sorry. I didn't know."

I shook my head at him. "No, it's just a bruise. There's nothing to do about it. Just wait for it to heal." With my pale skin, I knew the bruise probably stood out more.

He made sweeping looks at Victor and then at Silas. Silas was unreadable. Victor continued to twist the steering wheel as he drove. I quietly moved back into my seat, reaching for the belt to strap in.

Silas reached for my hand holding the belt buckle, stilling it. "You don't have to wear that if it hurts."

I shook my head. "It's not that bad. Really. You just surprised me."

He let go, allowing me to buckle in. I noticed he didn't strap himself in. I wondered if it was because he was so tall, it didn't fit.

"What I want to know is, how that guy got so close to you." Victor's baritone voice nearly rose an octave. "Wasn't she with you, Silas?"

"It's not his fault," I said. "He was taking care of the tray when Greg walked over."

"He had enough time to tell you his name and go with you down that hallway. What were you two doing in there?"

I blushed, touching my lower lip with my finger trying to remember. "I... I was going for the restroom. I went looking for you all, but didn't see you. I thought I'd slip into the bathroom where he couldn't follow me."

"You're probably lucky you didn't make it," Kota said. "If he was determined, he could have followed you in and if no one else was around..." He made a face and then he shook it off. "Next time just walk into the guy's bathroom if we're in there."

"No next time," Victor said. "We're not going to leave her by herself long enough to let 'Gregs' be a problem."

I wanted to cut in, but they sounded so angry with me. I wanted to bring my knees up and bury my head in them to hide the fact that I was blinking back tears. I forced myself to look out the window. The trees and buildings whizzed past and it was making me dizzy. There was no way I would let them see how upset I was. I was glad they were safe. I was unhappy that my first real adventure out turned into such a disaster.

The car fell into silence as Victor pulled into traffic on the drive home. At some point, I dared to look at the others. Victor was still fuming but he seemed intent on staring straight ahead at the road. Kota appeared busy with his phone.

Silas was glaring out the window. His jaw was set. His fist was clenched so tightly, he was crumpling the music book in the bag between us. I didn't want him to ruin Victor's music sheets. I reached over, placing a hand softly on his forearm.

Silas blinked, turned his head slowly and gazed down at me. I brushed my fingers over his fist, taking a hold of the other side of the bag. When he realized what he was doing, he forced his fist open. I took it from him and in an effort to ease the tension, tried to smile.

His eyes fell on my face. His lips parted until I could see his teeth and his cheeks flushed. He offered a return smile. It disappeared again. He turned back to the window.

I managed to calm myself a little, but was still worried about what everyone was thinking. Ideas ran through my head. They were thinking how terrible it was to invite this girl along. They wondered about the best way to ditch me, possibly ignoring me the whole semester.

I tried to quiet my thoughts but it was so upsetting to think I may have just lost the first friends I had ever come across. My parents wouldn't have to learn about this day and I wouldn't have to worry about telling them about anyone I'd met. No one would want to invite me over any more now. I wanted to say I was probably being paranoid this time, too. It wasn't working. Who wanted to bring a girl around who would attract trouble and needed to be babysat? I should have been the one to know what to do against unwanted attention.

While everyone was distracted, I smoothed out the slight crumple from Victor's book. The bag opened a little and I took a peek at the title.

Winter by Vivaldi.

♥♥♥

That night, I lay awake in my own bedroom on top of the covers on my bed, and staring at the ceiling light. I was probably burning out my eyes.

The car ride home had been completely quiet. Silas barely looked at me as he left the car. Victor dropped me off at my house before going to Kota's. His car was still parked in Kota's drive. I'd been at the window of my room a million times just to try to get a glimpse of them. There was a trail of ruffled mauve carpet between my window and my bed. I'd wondered if, at some point, I could take a walk outside, pass by Kota's house, and see if they noticed, but it seemed like such a stupid move. Would I look pathetic and needy when they were trying to just quietly tell me to keep my distance? I'd cried a little when I got home. My eyes felt cold and I probably looked like a mess. I wouldn't want them to see me like this.

I turned onto my side. My bed was pressed up against the wall near the closet. There was a small bookshelf against another wall, only half filled with worn novels. A green trunk sat under the window. The only odd part about the room was that, against the wall near the window, there was a small half door that led to some attic space.

The closet held only the small amount of clothes. My father usually bought clothes for us as my mother never went out. The selection that belonged to me was slight. I was smaller than my older sister, so we couldn't swap clothes. Sometimes she passed down a t-shirt or pair of jeans, but it was rare.

There wasn't a poster on the wall. No collection of photos. No decorations. The slightly faded pink flower wallpaper was a luxury compared to my last bedroom, which had stark white walls. I thought of Kota's bedroom and how similarly we kept the large space in the middle. I wondered what he would think of my room, and then found the thought pointless. He could never come to my bedroom, and as it was now, I wasn't sure if he would want to.

Before yesterday, my room felt like the only safe spot. If I stayed inside it, my mother couldn't complain and punish me. Now that I'd had a taste of freedom, of meeting people that were so nice to me, it felt more like a prison than ever. Despite the fight with Greg, thoughts ran through my head of the guys and how they made me feel. It was amazing. I wanted more.

The phone rang downstairs. I turned the music up a little on the stereo box at the foot of my bed.

"Sang!" My mother called out from downstairs. "Phone!"

My eyes shot open. A phone call. Me?

I dashed down the stairs, and thundered through the hallway into the kitchen. My mother stood barefoot on the tile, wearing a dingy mauve robe, her two-tone blond hair pulled back in a sloppy ponytail behind her head. She was shorter than I was, but broader shouldered and slouching. Her glassy blue eyes blazed at me. She started to hold the cordless phone to me but just before I touched it, she pulled it back, reconsidering her position.

"Who's calling you?" she asked me. Her voice was scratchy and sharp.

I shrugged. I really had no idea. "Might be from the school?"

She thought about it and slowly relinquished the cordless phone to me.

I nervously took the receiver. *Please just go back to your bedroom*, I thought. Her eyes shot lightning in my direction. I knew what was coming.

"Hello?" I said into the phone.

"It's Silas."

My heart fluttered so hard in my chest it was difficult to keep my feet on the ground. I tried to look unimpressed. My mother was still staring at me. "Hi," I said.

"I just wanted to make sure you got home safe."

The silence stretched between us. My head was rattling with what I could say to him that wouldn't set my mother off in a barrage of questions. "How did you know my number?"

"Kota had it."

Wouldn't Kota have told him I was okay? It made me wonder if there was another reason why he called and he'd made up an excuse. "Oh." I wanted to ask further but I didn't know how to phrase the question. How did Kota manage to get the number when I didn't even know it yet? My mother crossed her arms in front of her. Her scowl made creases at the corner of her mouth and around her eyes. *Oh please,* I thought, *not while I'm on the phone. I don't want Silas to hear.*

"He said I should wait to call. He said you were probably freaked out still from this afternoon and that we needed to give you a break."

Kota had told them to avoid me! "I... I'm fine."

"Who is it?" my mom said in a loud tone.

"It's the school," I said, loud enough for Silas to hear. My mom looked at me as if she didn't believe me, but stalked off back to her bedroom, or at least in that direction.

"Not safe to talk?" he asked.

"Uh huh," I said, again trying to sound bored and unimpressed, in case my mother was still listening, hoping Silas would understand.

"I won't be around tomorrow," he said. "I've got practice."

"That's okay." Was he thinking I would assume he would be around? Or would he have come over if he didn't have practice? His true meaning whirled around in my head. What was practice? I wanted to run to my room with the phone and shut everyone out, but doing it would look so suspicious.

"I'll talk to you later?" he asked.

There was a distinctive click and then the sound of breathing. My mother had picked up another phone and was listening in.

"Yeah," I said.

"'Bye," Silas said and hung up.

I held my breath, waiting and listening to the breathing on the line.

"Hello?" my mother's voice sounded like an echo in my ear because I could hear her from her bedroom as well as in the phone. "Who's on the line?"

I cringed and pulled it away from my face. I heard the line click again and then I switched off the phone.

"Sang! Come here!"

I shuddered where I stood, gently placing the receiver onto the cradle. I steeled myself, readying my lies.

Keeping friends was harder than I'd thought.

"Sang," my mother spat as she leaned on the edge of her bed. The mattress sagged under her weight. When I was around nine, my mother went to the hospital with a sinus infection, stayed for a month, came back with a bottle of morphine and has kept to her bed ever since. My parents never told us what was wrong with her, but I overheard whispers in their late evening discussions about her liver and pancreas. Sometimes at night she cried out in pain and my father took her to the hospital. She held her bottle of pills in her hands now, twisting her palm over the cap as if trying to remember when she took the last one.

"Yes?" I said in a near whisper. I stepped barefoot onto the cream carpet of her bedroom, doing my best to look bewildered. If I could only make her believe me this time.

"Who called you?"

"The school," I said. My eyes flitted to the light brown and ivy green wallpaper along the walls and the whirling wicker fan above her bed. Her eyes were too intense for me. "It was a reminder about registration."

Her thin lips pursed. She put her bottle of pills down and smoothed her chubby fingers over the covers of her quilt blanket. "It looked like you were trying to hide something."

I sighed. "I'm not used to getting phone calls."

"Why was it a man? Why did he only ask for you?" Her eyes narrowed at me, picking the holes at my story. "Why didn't he also ask about your sister?"

"I don't know," I said, my fingers fluttered to the base of my throat. "Maybe he'll call back for her in a minute. Or maybe it's because I'm younger..."

She chuffed. "No. You're lying. I don't think the school has our phone number." She stood up and then pointed a finger at me. "Who did you give this number to?"

My eyes widened and I took a step back, accidentally bumping into the wall. "No one! I don't even know our phone number."

"It sounds like a lie." She crossed the room toward me. "Why are men calling to talk to you?"

"I don't know!" I cried out, turning my face away from hers, pressing myself back against the wall. Please, no. Not now.

She grabbed my arm and started wrenching me until I was on my knees. I cried out in pain. "Who called you?" she asked through her teeth.

"The... school," I sobbed. What would she do to me? There was no way I was going to tell her about Silas. She could do what she wanted to me.

Her nose flared and I felt the sweat from her palms as

she pulled me up to my feet. I cried as she yanked me in to the kitchen. My heart was pounding and my body was shaking. Why wouldn't she just believe me this once? Why couldn't I call people like other girls?

"Get on your knees," she said.

I closed my eyes, wrapping my arms around myself and sunk to the floor. It wasn't uncommon for her to punish us by having us kneel on the floor for hours at a time. I thought this was one of those cases. If it had been, I would have been grateful.

She started moving around me, pulling vinegar from the shelf and lemon juice from the fridge. I didn't understand, but I kowtowed to her on the floor, crying. I whispered to the floor, pleading, under my breath, that she would stop and just send me to my room.

She created a concoction of half vinegar and half lemon juice in a glass and then handed it to me. "Drink all of this. You are never, ever to let a boy call here."

My lips trembled. "Please don't make me," I begged. Tears slid down my cheeks, dripping from my chin.

My mother reached for my hair, yanking it back until my face was up.

"Okay!" I screamed, "I'll do..."

The glass was pushed to my lips so hard I tasted blood at first as my lip split, and then all I could taste was the heat of the acid mix between lemon and vinegar. I forced myself to swallow, unable to catch a breath. If I didn't drink, I would drown.

The liquid slipped past my throat and I felt it burning. Out of instinct, my hands sought out her arms, trying to push her away. She held me in place until I drained the glass. When I was finished, and her hands released me, I collapsed to the ground in a heap. I choked, holding my palm to my mouth, gasping and sobbing so hard that I couldn't catch my breath. My lungs ached as I was trying to breathe and my throat was on fire. Every breath was painful to my throat.

She threw the glass into the sink and it shattered against the metal. "Next time a boy calls, it'll be bleach. Get up and go to your room. I don't want to hear from you." She stalked back to her bedroom and I heard her shaking her medicine bottle and opening the container.

I felt my stomach lurch. I pushed my palm to my mouth until I could run up stairs to the bathroom. I knelt at the toilet, my head buried in the bowl and I heaved.

When I was done, I fell on my back against the carpet of the bathroom. My body trembled and I tried breathing through my nose and mouth at different lengths but it was useless. Every little bit of air passing my throat made the pain sharply return. I forced myself to stop sobbing so it wouldn't hurt so badly. I got up, nearly crawling on my knees to the sink, dipping my head under the faucet for water, but the water's coolness sent me to my knees again as it splashed against my throat.

I sensed someone watching. Marie stood in the doorway. Through the tears in my eyes, I shuttered under my sister. Her brown hair hung long past her shoulders and her dark eyes looked curious and fearful.

"What was it this time?" she asked. I knew what she wanted. She wanted to make sure she never did what I had done.

I parted my lips, "Ah..." I coughed. "A boy..." I whispered. My eyes popped open. I tried again to talk. Nothing. I closed my eyes, and fresh, hot tears slid down my cheeks.

My mother had made sure I couldn't answer the phone.

NATHAN

I dreamed I was lost in a house I didn't know. There was a ghost behind me, rattling the windows and screeching so loud that I cowered in the corners to avoid it as it flew by my head.

I woke up in my bed, my heart pounding. When I calmed myself, I fell back into the pillow.

Ever since I was nine years old, I've had nightmares about monsters coming at me in the night. They take on different forms all the time. Sometimes it's hairy, brown tarantulas so big they could knock down trees as they chased me through a forest. Sometimes men in dark clothes with guns hunted for me in underground mazes. In every dream I had, I was running from something that didn't want me to exist, running toward a place I couldn't see. I taught myself not to cry out, so I wouldn't wake anyone else in the house.

Screaming was pointless; no one would come.

The next morning, I was out the door at dawn. It was a risk after the previous day, but I needed to escape. I needed fresh air. My throat no longer burned, but it was sore. I tested my voice a few times, but what I managed to say was raspy. It worried me that perhaps my voice was permanently damaged. I couldn't stand to think that was the case. I would be Sang, the girl with nothing to say, and no voice to say it.

I wore a pair of jeans and a simple pink blouse, ready to walk through the woods a million times to pass the hours. I wasn't sure if I should try to visit Kota. I'd been up half the night going over Silas's words. Kota had warned everyone to stand by to give me room to relax. Or had he meant to keep everyone away from me because they wanted to distance themselves from me? Which did he mean?

With no voice, I wanted to avoid him a little, too. How could I explain it? I wasn't sick. Or maybe I should pretend to be sick. It would be a good excuse. Only it wasn't possible. What if he tried to call? What if Silas tried to call again?

The morning air was already warm, and I breathed in the humidity. It felt heavy and thick as if I was walking through a lake I could breathe in. I wondered where that chill evening with the rain had gone. I almost regretted wearing jeans, but I didn't like to walk through the woods in shorts if I wasn't sure about the paths. I never knew when I would want to explore something off the trail, and would end up knee deep in underbrush.

The wood behind my parents' house was a couple of acres in size. There was another ravine behind Kota's house on the other side of the street, and I tried to find a way into that forest, but the empty lot was the only place to cross into it without walking through someone's yard. The lot had a cluster of trees so thick, though, I couldn't see a path into it.

I cut through the back yard and crossed a small wooden plank that served as a small bridge over a drainage ditch, separating the yard from the tree line. I disappeared behind the wall of trees, seeking out the footpath I had discovered the first afternoon my family had moved in.

There were a handful of trails in this forest and I had taken a few of them. I found one I hadn't tried yet and followed it. It wound around close to where I could see other homes along the street through the trees. The sunlight filtered through the leaves. The shadows from above cast an eerie green shade. I felt enclosed and separated from everything, which was wonderful in the moment. I didn't want to be seen. Fresh moss and pine scents filled my nose. A few mockingbirds were awake; one seemed to be following above me, calling out a tune that resembled a car alarm.

Along the path, a maple tree had fallen across the dirt trail. The broken limbs, many taller than me, blocked the way.

I considered going back, but the tree didn't look too dangerous. There was space between branches where I could climb through. I thought if I reached the center, I could probably get to the other side.

I started to pick my way through the branches. The leaves were still green, so it hadn't been down long. I wondered if it fell after the rain on the night I met Kota. My sneakers sunk into piles of soggy leaves and crunched the smaller branches.

When I was near the trunk, I gripped one of the thicker branches to step on top of the center and climb over it. I hesitated, trying to figure out my next move. The branch snapped, I lost my balance and grabbed it to steady myself. There was a loud crack, the sound echoing through the woods. I slipped, crashing into a mess. I reached instinctively, my hands flailing, trying to protect myself, feeling scratches from the branches. It spooked me so bad, that I cried out, which came out more of a raspy yelp.

I landed under some of the branches. I wasn't hurt, just surprised, but my heart was racing. I was shaking some leaves away from my head when a shout echoed to me.

"Someone over there?" It was a male voice, deep. Not as deep as Silas's and one I didn't recognize.

My heart started to pound and my eyes went wide. I couldn't let someone see me like this. Still, there wasn't an easy way out of the middle of this tree. If I tried to move, it wouldn't be quiet and he'd for sure hear me anyway.

"Yeah," I called out, but it was a stage whisper. I stood up, hunching over to avoid an overhanging branch.

I heard footsteps coming nearby. I scrambled to get out of the branches. One of them struck my face and stung my cheek.

The footsteps stopped short of the fallen tree. "Where?"

"In the tree," I screeched out. I coughed. Trying to yell to him irritated my throat.

"Didn't you see it was down? Why didn't you take the other path?" The footsteps came closer.

I found a thicker branch to stand on. I climbed for a short distance until I could see over most of the leaves. A guy with a stern face and serious blue eyes looked back at me. He wore a red and white Nike shirt, the sleeves cut off, and sport shorts in a matching red color. Earbud headphones hung around his shoulders. His hair was cut short, a mix between red and brown, leaning more on the red side. His chin was angled and his jaw was set as he looked at me. The expression was so solemn. This guy could mean business just by his look. He was about the same height as Kota but it was the bulk of his muscles that had my spine tingling. He had broad tapered shoulders and there was a power in his stature that was undefinable.

"Can you get out?" he asked. He dropped a hand onto his hip, with his head tilted toward me, and a baffled look on his face.

"I think so," I whispered, not trying to get too cocky with my predicament. I was already this far. I picked my way over branches and pushed away leaves from my face.

"What's wrong? Why are you whispering?"

I took a deep breath in and then patted my throat where he could see.

"Your voice broke?"

I partially smiled at the way he said it and nodded.

"Move left," he said.

I turned left, squinting my eyes to try to figure out what he was talking about because the branches were thick on that end.

"Shit, sorry. I meant my left. Your right."

I turned around and then pointed to the trunk, raising my eyebrows.

"Follow it down the tree until you get beyond the

branches," he motioned toward where the trunk had split, where the branches stopped. He maneuvered himself to walk around the edge of the tree, picking his way beyond the path to find where the tree limbs thinned out.

I followed his instructions, hanging on to tree branches, carefully this time. Using the trunk as a bridge, I shuffled my way over the limbs. It was a slow process, but I managed to get to the point where the tree trunk started to slant up . When I got there, I wasn't sure what to do.

"Can you climb up to the top?" he asked when he saw me starting to turn around. He was standing by the roots, a hand covering the top of his eyes as he looked at me against the sun.

I coughed and whispered as loud as I could, "What do you mean?"

"Just climb up here and then jump down."

I tried to judge the distance from where he was pointing. My heart started to thump again. Did he mean for me to jump from that high?

"You'll be fine. Come on."

My heart was thudding, but he seemed confident in his suggestion. I crouched a little on the trunk. Using my hands to help, I pulled myself up until I was out of the way of branches and I had a clear shot at the ground. I got up to a point where he was standing under me. He lifted his arms up, urging with his hands.

"Jump from there," he said.

I blinked at him. "Back up so I've got room," I whispered. I was already wary of the distance, but I'd had some training as a kid in elementary school on how to fall, so I thought I could tumble roll when I hit the ground.

"No, it's fine. I'll get you."

My mouth dropped open. He couldn't mean he was going to try to catch me when I jumped down. Wouldn't it hurt?

He smirked. "Will you just listen to me? Jump."

I hesitated again, swallowing and considering trying behind me where he wasn't able to reach.

"Fuck thinking. Thinking hurts the team. Jump."

My heart was thudding, but I lined myself up and leapt down to him. If he wanted to get hurt trying to soften my landing, I'd let him.

With his arms out, he seized me around the waist as I fell, and spun me a little to ease the momentum. My head was pressed up against his chest, and I breathed deeply from the adrenaline rushing through me. I inhaled a leather and Cyprus scent from him. My body shook against him.

He didn't let go. A hand came up at my back, holding me to him and he rubbed at my shoulders. His chin moved against my forehead so I felt the gruffness of coarse hair against his face. "It's okay. You're fine. You made it." He repeated himself a couple of times, softly and reassuring.

When I felt I could stand without falling over, I backed away. My face felt flushed and while my hands still shook, it became too awkward to hold on to him anymore. The moment was so intimate; I was embarrassed at having put myself in such a predicament. I didn't even know his name. "Thank you," I whispered. "You're okay, right?" I asked, swallowing after. I was worried I had hit something on him on my way down.

He nodded. His cheeks were tinted red but his face was back to that serious expression. "I'm okay. What made you think you could climb over it like that?"

"It didn't look too bad from the other side," I said, casting my eyes away. "I guess I just wanted to see if I could."

A small smile formed at the side of his mouth. "You're not really dressed for climbing like that."

At his mention of it, I checked myself over. I had a few scratches on my arm, but nothing was bleeding. My clothes were a little dirty, but everything seemed fine.

"What happened to your wrist?" he said, pointing to the bandage on my arm. The wound was scabbed over and I didn't really need the bandage. It just looked ugly, so I opted to cover it up.

"I fell a couple days ago," I whispered. How many

C. L. Stone

times would I need to explain my injuries? It made me hyper sensitive to dare to put another bandage on myself. I'd have to repeat myself so much.

"You're accident prone. Come on," he said. "Let's get out of here."

He took my hand and led the way around the tree until we were on the other side where the path started again. When we were safe, he let go of me. I was grateful that he let go because I was nervous, but I was also sad. His hand felt comforting.

"How long has the tree been down?" I asked in a whisper.

He looked at me, raising his eyebrows. He leaned over me, bringing his ear close to my face. "What?"

His reddish hair looked soft, like rabbit fur. My fingers itched to touch, but I knew I never would. I swallowed to try to gain some of my voice back and repeated myself.

"A week, I think," he said. "I keep meaning to come back out here to clear it out from the path, but I've been putting it off. There was a bad storm before you moved in."

I blinked at him, my hand on my upper stomach, rubbing at where a branch had scratched me. "You know who I am?"

"I've seen you around." He ran his fingers through the longer bits of hair on the top of his head. "I'm Nathan."

"Sang."

He blinked at me and then leaned in closer.

"My name is Sang," I rattled off.

"Sang?"

I nodded.

He smiled, the blue of his eyes softening. "I'm two houses down from you. Same side." He waved at the direction our houses were. "Want me to walk you back?"

The question surprised me. He was being nice. Another person that could be a friend. My head swirled with the suddenness of it. At the same time, I was resistant. It felt like I was pressing my luck. The more people I tried to be friends with, the bigger the chance my parents would find out. I'd get

70

myself into trouble. "I don't mean to ruin your jog." It was the politest thing I could say to decline.

He shrugged. "It's nothing." He motioned to the path. "Comin'?"

I pushed a finger to my lower lip but I started after him. I couldn't say no without sounding mean. Part of me didn't want to. He was handsome and sweet and he had helped me. How could I refuse?

The path left enough room that we were walking side by side. "You're going to the public school, right?" he asked.

I nodded.

"About time we had someone new around here. There's only a handful of kids on this street."

"I haven't seen them around."

"You will," he said, swaying his arms a little as he strolled along beside me.

I raised an eyebrow at him, curious as to what he meant.

He grinned, understanding my expression. "You've got the good basketball goal."

I tried to remember where the basketball goal was. "The one hanging from the garage," I whispered. It had been there when we moved in.

"Yeah. Full height and that wide driveway that's at least half court, I think," he smirked. "Don't laugh, but I came over one night to jump on it, just to see if I could hang from it."

I did smile but stopped myself from giggling. "It's still there, so you must have made it."

He nodded. "It's pretty strong."

I admired the muscles in his arms, and what I could see of his chest. He looked pretty sturdy. It must have been true about the basketball goal, if he was able to hang off of it.

"So what happened to your voice?"

I opened my mouth to respond to him but I wasn't sure how.

"You're not sick, are you?" he asked, his eyebrow going up. "I'm not going to catch something, am I?"

I didn't want to worry him, so I shook my head.

C. L. Stone

He smirked. "You've been talking too much, huh?" he asked. "Girls always talk too much."

I tried to shoot him a friendly smirk back. It was a better solution than the truth.

We turned a bend and I started to recognize we were coming up along where the path split. He had taken me back around to where I had started.

"You go for walks this early in the morning a lot?" he asked.

I twisted my mouth a little, unsure how to answer. "I couldn't sleep and I hadn't followed this path yet, so I came to check it out."

He looked at me. "Did you try the woods on the other side of the street yet?"

"No. How do you get over there?"

He smiled. "I'll show you. It's a little easier to get lost over there though and there's some things you should see. Like there's a big ditch you may not see walking up to. I think that's how they drained the land around here, so they could develop it."

I grinned, nodding to him. I understood. I swallowed. "I'll check it out."

He gave me a side glance and smirked again. "On second thought, I ought to go with you over there. Don't go without me."

I angled my head toward him. "I'd be fine."

"Uh huh," he said. He stopped walking and turned toward me. He reached over my head and pulled a maple leaf from my hair. "You'll be fine, unless there's a fallen tree."

My face heated up. I started to shake my head, my mouth moving trying to figure out the best way to say I would have gotten out eventually.

"Think you could do it alone? As you wish. Next time I'll leave you," he said, letting the leaf fly from his hand to the ground and starting off down the path again.

I stepped quickly up next to him, matching his stride. Something about him made me want to stick around. He seemed so cool. I wanted him to like me. "How do you get

72

over there?" I whispered.

"Nope. I'm not telling you now."

I frowned, my lip pouting.

He made a face and then pulled his fingers over his lips, zipping.

"Ugh," I grumbled. "I'll figure it out."

"Sure."

I rolled my eyes.

He stopped short along the path at a place where the trees started to thin out, giving us a view of the back of some homes. He pointed to an opening in the trees. Another slab of wood was nestled into the ground over a ditch, and on the other side was a wide wood fence. I had missed it the first time, but there was a latch and handle sticking out of one of the wood planks. It took me a moment to see the frame of the door. "This is my stop," he said.

I caught the scent of chlorine and a hint of sparkling aqua blue between the gaps in the fence. "You have a pool?"

He hesitated and then nodded.

I grinned and felt my heart lifting. "Is it big?"

My enthusiasm seemed to catch him off guard. "Come and look at it. You tell me." He headed toward the plank.

I followed him. When he got to the wood piece, he crossed it halfway and then reached out for my hand. "Or do you want to do it yourself?"

I made a face but reached for his hand. He took mine in his grasp, holding on to me as he moved forward. I followed on his heels. My heart fluttered as his hand was big, wrapping easily around mine. He let go when we were both on the ledge on the other side and he moved to open the gate.

What yard there might have been in the back of his house was taken up by a large shed close to the fence. Beyond that was a rectangular pool, at least twenty-five feet long. The edges were curved and the water rippled, sparkling in the sunlight. A large beige concrete patio surrounded it, looking almost like sand.

I stepped up to the edge of the pool, looking down into the water. If I was a cat, I would have been purring. Before my mother got sick, she took Marie and me to the pool to learn how to swim. When I was in seventh grade, the school had a pool, and during gym for a whole month, I got to swim in it. I had missed the scent of chlorine and the feel of the water flowing around me as I swam.

"How deep is it?" I asked, forgetting that I was probably whispering and wasn't sure if he could hear me. My eyes locked on the sparkle of the water from the sun, dazzling me.

I heard him step up behind me and I felt the hand on my back, but even then I wouldn't have imagined he would have pushed. I found myself flying and I hit the water.

At first the water had a crispness to it but my skin quickly adjusted to the temperature, so that it was actually very comfortable. The sharp taste of chlorine swept into my mouth. I touched bottom after about six feet and then slowly rose to the top. A splash hit the water nearby. Nathan smoothly touched the bottom with a palm. His shirt and shoes were off. When his head and chest rose out of the water, I was in awe of the muscles that were defined in his body. Unlike Silas, whose bulk of muscle was smooth, Nathan was a precision machine. The ripples of muscles along his abdomen fit together like a living puzzle.

A smile broke on his lips as those penetrating blue eyes fixed on my face. "Did you find out?"

I was grinning like a crazy girl. I didn't care that he pushed me in at all. I pushed a hand against the surface of the water to splash him.

He ducked his head away, lifting an arm in a half effort to protect himself. "Hey there, little mermaid. You don't want to start that game with me. I win every time."

I pulled a face and did another splash, smaller, but still defiant.

"As you wish." He was gone under the water again.

With the bulk of my jeans and being weighed down by my sneakers, I couldn't move fast enough on the surface to break away from him. His arms enveloped my waist. My heart was furiously beating in my chest as I felt this touch. He lifted me out of the water onto his shoulder. He waited just a moment, and then tossed me back into the water like I was nothing but a doll.

I landed with another splash not far from where he was. When I broke the surface again, I was giggling, flicking water away from my eyes. He laughed too, swimming closer to me.

I shook my head, holding up my hands in defeat. "Not fair." I pointed to the jeans and shoes I had on that were weighing me down.

"Take them off."

My mouth dropped open. "What? No!" I screeched.

"Then lose." He inched toward me, deliberately teasing with his grin and wiggling his fingers at me.

I took one shoe off, flinging it toward the side of the pool. It landed with a thick thud against the concrete. The other one joined it a moment later.

"I'm not taking my pants off," I whispered.

He stood there laughing, his hands on his hips. "You'll wear a bikini that has less material than you're wearing now with that shirt and you won't take your pants off. You are wearing underwear, right?"

I hated to tell him that I'd never worn a bikini. I inched back a little where I could stand on my toes. With my jeans on, it took a lot more energy just to stay afloat. "Yeah..."

"You could run back to your house and grab your bathing suit, I guess."

There was a problem with that. Sneaking back in, soaking wet, would definitely draw attention, and there was no way I could get back out again. Besides that, I couldn't remember if I had a bathing suit; I hadn't been swimming for years. If I ran away and never came back, he wouldn't understand. It really wasn't an option, if I wanted him to like me, and I did.

I felt for my pants button and started to undo them.

"No!" he called out, holding up a hand to me and laughing. "Stop it." He swam to the edge of the pool and got out. He came around to where I was close to the edge and motioned to me. "Come on. I've got an old pair of shorts that might fit you. If you tie them, they'll probably be okay."

I moved to the edge of the pool, intending to get out on my own, but he grabbed me under my shoulders, pulling me up out of the water. He plopped me down next to him, holding me steady again to make sure I was on my feet before letting go.

I was breathless. He stepped away from me toward the house. I wanted to fall over. My heart was about to explode. He was strong, nice, and funny. I couldn't think straight. Another friend. What was I getting myself into? The more people I met, the more disappointed I was going to be when they found out who I really was and rejected me. Weird. No sense of how to behave around people. All I had to rely on was what I'd read in books, and so far it wasn't helping much.

Nathan disappeared into the house. I moved under the overhang of the back porch and toward the sliding glass door he had gone in. The house was one story, with brown and beige brickwork and I half remembered what it looked like from the street. What it lacked in height, it made up in sprawl. From the doorway, I could see into a living room with a high, white ceiling and exposed beams. The floor was a gray stone tile. The walls were white. The furniture was dark brown and leather. It reminded me of a cabin that I'd seen once on television. There was a musky smell, like a mix of the leather and the lacquer in the wood fixtures.

Nathan returned from a hallway beyond the living room. He held a pair of green shorts in his hands. He moved to the door, bending his head to look down at me. "Want to come in?"

I made a face, pointing to my wet clothes. "I'm dripping," I whispered.

"So am I." He pulled the sliding door open further and beckoned to me. "There's a bathroom right there. You can put the shorts on if you want."

I nodded.

"Do you want a t-shirt?" he asked. "It'll probably be big on you."

76

I tugged at my blouse. "It'll give time for this to dry."

He smiled. "I'll toss them in the dryer after you're done."

He pointed me toward the bathroom again and I stepped inside of it. There didn't appear to be anyone else around. My parents would have killed me if they'd known I was alone with a boy in an empty house. As it was, my own mind was coming up with all the things my parents warned me about. Would he have me follow him to his bedroom? Would he pressure me for sex? Would I be interested? And why did I feel like I was betraying Kota, Silas and Victor by being here? Were they worried about me right now and wondering what was going on? Did they even care? Maybe I needed Nathan after all. If I messed up too badly with Kota and the others, maybe Nathan and I could be friends instead. Were we friends now?

The bathroom was big. There was a wide tub with a glass sliding door. Black stone tile covered the floor, and the counter was carved dark stone. The walls were white. Photos of helicopters lined the walls.

I was just putting on the shorts when there was a knock at the door. "I've got a shirt."

I opened the door and he handed me a dark blue t-shirt with some writing in a language I didn't recognize.

"Does your dad fly helicopters?" I asked. My voice was weaker. What little ability I had gained to talk was becoming lost.

"Yeah," he said. I closed the door again. It sounded like he leaned against the door. "He makes trips between here and New York. Sometimes to Florida. He's gone a lot."

I picked up my wet clothes from the floor, holding them away from my body as they were dripping. I opened the door.

Nathan was against the door frame, leaning his head against it. He stood up straight as I took a half step out "It fits?" he asked.

The shorts were tied tight around my waist but the lower hem was down at my knees. The t-shirt was a couple of sizes too big and covered my butt. "I look weird."

77

He laughed. "You're actually kind of cute. You should totally wear that your first day of school."

I narrowed my eyes at him, but betrayed myself by giggling.

He took the wet clothes from my hand. "Go jump in. I'll put these in the dryer."

I crossed the living room, went outside and stepped up to the edge of the pool again. The smell of the chlorine was intoxicating. I wondered for a moment if he felt I was intruding on him for his pool. I had already interrupted his run. What other plans could I have been interrupting?

I did a shallow dive from one corner and took off across the water. Despite my worries, I wasn't going to waste a moment of swim time if I had his permission. Holding my breath, I wriggled my body to make my way to the opposite corner on the far end. I wanted to check to see how long I could hold my breath before getting up on the other side.

I almost made it. I blamed jumping in first and being so excited as to why I couldn't do it. I surfaced a couple of feet away, sucking in a breath of air and starting a slow breaststroke. When I reached the corner, I stopped for a moment and relaxed to slow down my breathing. I knew being calm under the water was important to being able to hold my breath longer. I pushed off with my feet against the edge of the pool.

I used my hands this time under the water to give me a little extra push, but most of the power came from the movements I made, almost mermaid-like. I cut through the water quickly, reaching the other side. I touched the far wall and popped up at the surface, taking in a breath.

"You could get faster," Nathan said. He was standing on the edge of the pool in front of the house. I almost smiled at him, ready with a joke that I knew he wouldn't be able to hear. I wanted to break the tension because he'd startled me. His face was serious. "Pull your hands to your chest." He did the motion with his own hands. "Shoot them out above your head as you do that thing where you bring your head up. Then as you're moving your feet, spread out your hands and pull like you're crawling through the water."

I watched his arm motions and then nodded. It didn't look difficult. I sucked in a breath and kicked off.

While I wasn't trying to go at my fastest speed before, knowing he was watching now, I threw my body into the motions. My body curved against the water and I tried the hand movement he'd shown me. It was more work forcing my arm muscles into sweeping motions, but he was right; the stroke was much more powerful and the effort was twice as effective.

I broke the surface at the far corner, hearing him hooting.

"You're good," he said.

I was breathless, but I smiled at him. I moved a hand to my arm, rubbing the bicep. It was going to be sore tomorrow if I kept up that pace.

"You should do some weight training." He walked over to where I was against the edge of the pool and slid in to stand next to me. He tilted his head at me. "Are you going to join the swim team?"

I blushed, shaking my head. "I'm not much of a competitor."

"You're shitting me."

I half laughed. "I don't mind a short race."

He blinked at me, smiling. "Should we race?" he asked.

Race him? He had to be kidding. "I'll try," I whispered.

"Should we bet on the outcome?"

My eyes narrowed at him. "You'll win."

"You don't know that. You're pretty quick. You're smaller than me, too. You could probably move through the water faster than I could."

"What do you want?"

He shrugged. "If you win, what would you want?"

I raised an eyebrow at him, unsure of his motives. Was this a trick to get me to do something else crazy? "I want to know the secret to getting into the back woods."

His mouth broke into a wide grin. "I was going to show you that anyway."

79

I made a face. I didn't know what else to ask for. Then I pointed to the t-shirt I was wearing. "This?" When I said it, it seemed to be too much. Was he being serious at all about it though? Or was this just for fun?

He nodded. "If I win..." he paused, looking at my face like he was trying to read something from me. I got the feeling he was weighing out what he could get away with asking me. "If I win, you promise that if we end up with a class together, you'll sit next to me."

It was an odd request. I felt my brows lifting. I wasn't sure if he was serious. "That's it?" I croaked out.

"Hey, if I'm going to cheat off of someone, I'd like a willing participant."

My mouth popped open and my fingers flutter to the base of my throat. "Nathan?"

He shook his head, laughing. "I'm kidding. I don't cheat."

I grinned. "I do." There was no way I could win this race. I knew he wouldn't let me. I positioned my feet up against the edge of the pool.

The smile remained on his face and he tilted his head toward me. "Really?"

Before he reacted, I shot away from the wall under the water, pushing myself against the resistance with what strength I had inside me. I managed to get past him and tried to widen the distance to be out of his reach. I used the arm movement he showed me, throwing my whole body into the stroke. If I was going to have a chance, I needed to get clear of him.

I was halfway through the pool when I felt a hand on my ankle. In one pull, I was sailing backward through the water faster than I'd ever moved at my own doing. Nathan flew ahead of me. His reddish hair broke the surface and in a few easy breaststrokes, he was on the other side.

I made it over halfway again before I surfaced. I bobbed in the water, my chest heaving as I was laughing too hard. "Cheat!" I gasped out.

"You can't cheat if you didn't set rules." He stood up,

drips of water sliding over the muscles in his chest and stomach. I tried not to gape but it was hard not to be in awe of the power he had.

I made a face at him, sticking my tongue in his direction.

"Don't go pulling that face on me. You owe me now."

I laughed, splashing him. I didn't think I would have minded sitting next to him in class, anyway. Although when I thought about it, I wondered how I would concentrate if I had someone like him nearby.

He smirked, sizing me up and positioning his legs against the wall. "I warned you about splashing."

He caught me before I had a chance to move.

It was another hour before I crawled my way out of the pool, falling on my stomach on the concrete, gulping in air.

"Give up?" Nathan asked, coming up beside me and sitting on the edge of the pool with his legs in the water.

"You play rough," I wheezed out. Between all the races and him tossing me around the pool, I was dizzy.

He laughed and shook his head, rubbing a palm at his temple. "And here I thought I had my own little mermaid who could keep up," he challenged.

I blushed. Was he claiming me? "You know she dies at the end of the original story."

His eyes darkened and his lips twisted. "What? Why?"

"She sacrifices herself for the prince's happiness."

"That's fucked up. Wasn't he happy with her?"

"He was in love with another girl."

"What an ass."

I rolled my eyes and then flopped over until I was on my back, letting the sun warm me. There was a gentle breeze that flitted around us. I remained jealous of the pool he owned. Whenever I could own my own house, I decided I wanted one just like it.

His eyes focused on my body. I thought that he was being perverted for a moment as the shirt was sticking to my chest but I felt the breeze on my skin and then realized my side must have been exposed. The bruise near my butt was

81

prominent.

"Where'd you get that?" His eyes focused in on it. He reached out as if to touch it but he only lifted the shirt a little to get a better look. He sucked in a breath and then reached for his other hand to pull down the fabric of the shorts, leaning in to get a closer look. "Jesus. What'd you do that for?"

"I fell," I said softly.

"On to someone's foot?"

"On to the concrete."

"How the hell did it get that bad on your hip?"

"It was the angle, I think." I moved a hand to pull away the shirt and stuff it down to hide the bruise. "It's fine," I recited. "Looks worse than it feels."

"Probably not," he said. "I've had my share of bruises. That's a nasty one."

I shrugged and swallowed to try to get some voice back. "I can't do anything for it."

He pushed himself up until he was standing and then reached a hand down to me. "I've got something."

I wasn't sure if this was another trick, but I'd gotten sort of used to his face. When he wore that serious look, he meant it. Then I hesitated, because he was asking me to touch him again. I reached up, feeling his hand wrap around mine and he pulled me up until I was standing.

He held on to my hand, walking around the pool and heading toward the large shed that was in the back. It made me blush that he was holding my hand. We'd just met. He was touching me. Was this normal to happen right away? I mean, friends hold hands sometimes. I was sure I'd read about it in books. It also happened when a guy liked you a lot and wanted to be your boyfriend. So which was it? Why did these things have to be so confusing?

"Wait here," he said. "The floor is wood. I don't want you to slip."

"What about you?"

He ignored the question, or didn't hear me that time, and opened the latch, pulling open the wide barn-like door.

The inside of the shed did have a pine floor. The polish gleamed. There was black padding along the edges about a foot high against the wall and karate posters above them. There were a few belts in cases in different colors, dates etched into gold plates in the frames. A skylight at the top let in some natural light but he flicked a switch and two rows of fluorescent lights turned on.

I knew he said not to, but I couldn't resist wanting to get a closer look at the belts and posters on the wall. There was his name, Nathan Griffin, etched into those gold plates with the various degrees of rank that I didn't quite understand. There was a framed newspaper clipping with his name on it, too, and a picture of a much younger Nathan holding up a trophy. I sensed him stepping up behind me, looking at what I was looking at. "You do karate?" I asked.

"Kind of."

I turned to face him, blinking, not understanding.

"It's Jujitsu. And Taekwondo. And some other martial arts. Karate is just a different style."

"Oh," I said. "That's really cool."

His face softened and he smiled at me. "I know." He crossed the room to a small closet that protruded from the rear wall. He searched the shelves until he found what he was looking for and turned around. "Let me see that bruise again," he said, coming back across the floor.

I stepped back out onto the pavement and he turned off the light, closing the door. He turned to me and I lifted the shirt to reveal the bruise. He held a crumpled white tube in his hand. He opened the top and squirted out a white cream onto his palm. He pressed his fingers to the bruise to lather it into my skin.

"What is this?" An acidic medicine smell made me crinkle my nose. The cream was greasy and while he was delicate as he rubbed, it did hurt as he touched me. Part of me wondered if it was because I was super sensitive that he was a boy I still didn't know well, and he was touching a part of me that made me shiver.

"Arnica cream. It's supposed to help with bruising and

83

sore muscles." He dipped his fingers down into my shorts to cover a little more of the area, then wiped his hand off on his trunks and closed the medicine. He handed the tube to me. "Put this on twice a day until it starts to turn green."

I took the medicine and held it to my chest. "Thank you."

He was standing close to me. His blue eyes fixed on mine. "You're pretty nice for a girl."

I half choked. "What?"

"You know," he said, waving his hand around his head, being dismissive. "Girls are all 'give me that' and usually want to get all cute on the couch and not get their hair wet and... yeah, indoor types."

I lifted an eyebrow. "Girls don't like wet hair?"

He laughed. "You're totally missing the point."

"Probably because I'm a girl." I don't know why but I felt defensive about being separated from other girls. Normal girls don't like to swim?

He rolled his eyes, waving his hand again in the air, but laughed. An alarm noise sounded nearby and he raced over to where he had dropped his shirt near the pool. He pulled out a cell phone and answered it. I was trying not to overhear the conversation, but it was difficult not to. "Yeah? No, I was just swimming with Sang. She's the... oh. You know her?" He turned, looking at me with his eyebrow raised as he listened. "Yeah, okay. We'll come over." He hung up.

I swallowed. *Uh oh.* That had to be Kota or one of the other guys. So they knew each other?

He checked the sports watch at his wrist. "Have to be somewhere?"

I considered what I should say. Should I lie and go home? No, I still had to ensure they didn't try calling. I still wasn't sure how to explain what happened to my voice or why they couldn't do something as normal as call me. I shook my head.

Nathan's head tilted toward the house. "Let's get dressed. How'd you meet Kota?"

"Long story."

He smiled. "Tell me on the way to his house."

♥♥♥

I stood with Nathan on Kota's front porch. My hair was still wet and my jeans were kind of dirty. I was grateful they were fully dry. I pulled my hair out of the mess on top of my head, untangling the clip. I held the clip with my teeth and twisted my hair again, clipping it back up in a quick movement. Drips fell on my neck as the tips of my hair spilled out from the top of the clip.

Nathan watched me as I did it. "Looks like shit," he said with a teasing grin.

I made a face at him just as Jessica opened the door. She looked cute in a little pink flower dress. She peered out at us, took one look at Nathan, turned bright red and rushed away from the door, leaving it hanging open.

I lifted an eyebrow and turned toward him.

He looked perplexed at me and shrugged his shoulders. "She caught me sparring with a friend one day. It probably looked like I beat him up pretty bad. I heard Victor tell her one day if she didn't get straight A's like her brother, I'd come over and do the same thing to her."

I was still laughing when Kota came to the door.

"There you are," he said. He wore Calvin Klein jeans and a short sleeve, white dress shirt, buttoned to his neck. His slid his glasses up further on his nose, looking relieved. "What happened to you?"

I blinked at him. "You were looking for me?" I whispered.

His eyes focused on me. "What?"

"Her voice is gone," Nathan said. "She can't talk."

Kota's expression changed, his eyebrow raised. "It was fine yesterday. What happened?" His eyes were intense on me.

My heart was throbbing so hard that I wasn't sure how to react. My lips moved, but I couldn't figure out what to say.

He frowned. "I almost went over to your house. I wasn't sure how to reach you. I tried walking by just in case you

85

happened to look out. I wondered if you were in trouble."

I pushed a finger toward my lower lip. "Sorry," I whispered. I wasn't sure what else to say.

"What's the problem?" Nathan asked, shifting on his feet and looking between me and Kota. "What's going on?"

Kota fumbled with the button at the collar of his shirt. "Well, it's something we've got to figure out. Come on in. I'll look at your throat."

My hand fluttered to my throat, touching delicately the dip at the base. "It's not a problem," I whispered, forcing a smile. The last thing I wanted was this sort of complication. It was my responsibility to act as a barrier between my parents and anyone I met. If I was going to keep any friends at all, I had to stop them from discovering my problems at home.

How was I going to keep this peace, this separation of my friends and my family?

GABRIEL

trembled as I followed Kota through his house. Nathan closed the door behind us and fell in behind me. I could only catch a glance, but there were a ton of family photos on the walls, decorations in displays, rugs spread across the floor, and knickknacks on tables through the foyer. Compared to my own empty house, it felt almost cluttered, but I loved it. It felt so full and lived in. The living room had a blue carpet that was similar to the one in Kota's room. There was a beige sofa with plump embroidered pillows. A wide screen TV sat inside an entertainment center. There were a couple of plants sitting on top of side tables and a bookshelf along one wall filled with novels.

"Where's your mom?" I asked in my cracking voice, trying to pull the conversation away from me.

"She's at work." He looked at the sofa as if considering it. "We should head up to my room. But keep an ear out. Victor and Gabriel should be here in a minute."

I looked at Nathan, wanting to ask who Gabriel was, but he wasn't looking at me and instead headed off after Kota past the dining room, toward the start of the stairs.

I slowly followed them, trying to come up with something to tell them that wasn't the truth, or to make it lighter than what was going on. Only, my mind went blank. I'd already been not fully honest about other things. Did I really want to make some of my first friends here hate me because I lied to them? How would I ever explain my mom?

At the top of the stairs in his room, Kota started to drag his computer chair across the floor. He opened a side drawer at his desk, picking up a flash light. He positioned the chair in the middle of the room and then pointed at it. "Sit."

The command and power in his voice caused a knee-jerk reaction. I sank into the chair, unsure of what else I could do.

Kota stood in front of me, with Nathan beside him. They bent over me. Kota held the flashlight toward my face, flicking the light on. "Open up," he said.

I swallowed, opening at his request. Kota squinted through his glasses as he looked into my throat. He studied my mouth. I wasn't sure what I was supposed to do. My heart was pounding.

"What's wrong with her?" Nathan asked next to him. He was trying to glance around Kota's head to look inside my throat, too.

"It's... burned," he said. He flicked the light off. With his free hand he tugged at my chin, making me look at his eyes. "What happened yesterday when you got home?"

I moved my lips as the power in his voice lured me to, but I couldn't find the words. I was unable to lie to him. Was it his devouring green eyes, or the way his concern for me was apparent on his face?

Kota frowned. He knelt in front of me, wrapping his warm fingers around mine. "Sang, I'm going to assume if you're not telling me, it's something bad. I'm going to ask you some questions. Just nod if I'm right. Did you get into trouble yesterday with your parents?"

I sighed, nodding.

"Was it because you left with us?"

I shook my head. Nope.

Nathan sat on Kota's bed. I felt him looking at me, but I couldn't make myself face him.

Kota grasped my hand a little tighter. "Did they have you drink something?"

I bit my lip, closed my eyes and nodded. I swallowed hard. This was it, I thought. They would send me home now and I'd never see them again. Who wants to deal with a girl with crazy parents?

"What was it?" Kota asked softly. When I didn't respond, he squeezed my hand again. "Sang? Tell me. What was it?"

I peeled my lips apart to whisper. "Lemon juice... and vinegar."

"Fucking shit," Nathan bellowed. "What the hell did they do that for?" His eyes were so cold. He turned to Kota. "We have to do something. They can't do that."

"I know," Kota started. His eyes were fixed on me and his face was as serious as Nathan's. "Has this happened before?"

I shook my head.

"Why did they do it this time?"

I glanced at Nathan to divert my eyes somewhere besides Kota's face but Nathan was making me tremble just as badly. "Silas called," I whispered. "A boy's never called before. Please don't tell him. He'll feel bad. It's not his fault."

Nathan grunted. "Start at the top. Are you telling me I can't come for you if you're at your house? I can't call you? How bad are we talking?"

The sound of a car driving up and a short car honk cut through. *Ugh, more people*, I thought. Victor and Gabriel. This was way too complicated. I wanted to go home and hide, only I wasn't brave enough to move. Now Gabriel, a complete stranger, was going to learn about this, too. I shook with humiliation.

I hesitated and Kota stared at me a moment but then he got up. "Your voice will come back. You just need to rest your throat. Hang on a second." He crossed the room and ran down the stairs. I heard him answering the door below.

The moment he was gone, Nathan turned to me. "Why don't you just say it? Do your parents beat you?"

I waved my hands in the air across my body. "It's not quite like that. They don't hit me or anything."

"But they don't like you hanging out with anyone?

What happens if I show up?"

"Don't. Please."

His mouth turned into a frown. "Would they flip out if they found out you were with me today?"

I nodded.

"Hey," he said, he leaned toward me until his face was close to mine. "Don't worry. I won't say anything to them. What about the other girl? You have a sister, right? Did she get this, too?"

I shook my head. I slid out of the office chair and onto my knees to sit on the floor, sitting delicately on my heels. "She didn't have to drink..." I said, but my voice fell then. I swallowed.

Nathan moved off of the bed and then sat next to me. He was about to say something when thudding on the stairs sounded again. I heard someone shut the door downstairs and the flick of the lock and then three heads appeared as they got to the top of the stairs. Victor was first. He was wearing dark designer jeans this time; his shirt was white, buttoned up to his collarbone. His face looked a little strained, but when he saw me, he relaxed a little. He pushed his wavy hair back away from his eyes. Kota followed behind him. A moment later, another guy popped up from the stairs, looking as if he'd jumped the last couple of steps.

When I first heard the name, I thought it would be a girl. Gabriel was about Victor's height, though a little slimmer in the hips. His hair hung long around his chin, but was brushed back away from his face. Two locks of hair, one tucked behind each ear, were colored a light shade of blond. The rest of his hair was a rich brown. His eyes were crystal-like, bright blue, excited and wild. He had a couple of rings on each of his hands and stud earrings in each ear, his right had three more rings going up along the top. He wore jeans and a neon green tank shirt which showed off lean, but defined biceps.

"Oy," Gabriel said, his voice surprising me as it was deeper than Victor's. "So you're the troublemaker."

Heat radiated at my cheeks. Was that what they were

saying about me?

Victor gave him a chop on his head. "Don't pick on her."

Gabriel ducked away from Victor's hand and then moved to sit next to me. "Hey, I was only teasing," he said. "I didn't mean anything by it." He turned to me. "Don't listen to me, okay?" His face was so bright and happy. He had an angular chin, a slight nose and shaped eyebrows. His crystal blue eyes were dazzling like sunlight in pool water.

Kota tucked his chair back toward his desk and then sat across from us. Victor plopped down on Kota's bed, hands tucked behind his head, and looking up at the ceiling.

"We need to be more careful around her parents," Nathan said.

Kota nodded. "I think that's why we need to talk about it." He looked at me. "Tell us what we need to do."

I blinked at him, not sure what to say. What was this? They seemed to freely accept that my parents were difficult, and now they were willing to learn how to handle this? This seemed impossible. Anyone normal would have told me to go home and wouldn't want to get in the middle of it. I flitted looks from Kota's green caring eyes, to Nathan's serious expression, to Gabriel's curiosity... I even caught Victor turning his head, looking at me, and the fire in his eyes was a little subdued but working, as if thinking.

"I'm not sure where to start," I whispered. Did Victor and Gabriel know? Did Kota tell them?

The guys looked at each other. Gabriel and Nathan had that same knack of being able to read the others. There was the slight incline of the head from each of them before they turned back to me. "What would we have to do if we wanted to come over?" Kota asked. "Let's start with that."

As soon as the words were spoken, a thudding sound started to reverberate from the quiet of the neighborhood. A basketball was being bounced outside in the street.

Looks were exchanged between all of us. Nathan jumped up and rushed to the window seat, leaning against the frame to look outside. "It's Derrick."

Everyone else got up at once. Kota and I stood on either side of Nathan and looked down into the street. Victor and Gabriel moved to the other window to look out.

A guy about our age was walking up the street. His hair was black with a bowl cut. He was tan and wore jean shorts with no shoes, his removed shirt draped over his shoulder. He bounced a basketball with his hands as he walked down the street.

"Where is he going?" Nathan wondered out loud.

We watched in silence together as the boy walked to my house and started to head up the drive.

My eyes widened. What was he doing?

Kota caught my hand that was fluttering at my throat, enclosing it with both of his hands. "Did you meet him? Is he going to ask for you?"

I shook my head, watching as the boy disappeared into the open garage attached to the house toward the side door. "I've never seen him before."

He let go of my hand. I think we were all holding our breath, waiting for whatever was going to happen.

After what felt like eons, the boy reappeared. Marie trailed behind him, slow, hesitant.

They started playing basketball.

I blinked. My sister was playing with the boy down the road. What was she doing?

"Looks okay to me," Nathan said. He turned to me. "Maybe we should go over."

"Wait a minute," I said, taking a hold of his shirt sleeve to stop him before he could leave. He looked at me and then back out at the house.

It only took a few minutes. They were trading off the basketball in what looked like a game of HORSE or PIG. The ball was tossed at the goal. Marie started to run for it but stopped dead. They turned their heads toward the garage. My sister ducked her head and ran for the garage. The boy collected his basketball and started his way back down the drive.

"What happened?" Nathan turned to me. "Was it your

mom?"

I nodded. "She called to them at the door." I watched as the boy made his way back up the road. "*You should go home. She has chores to do,*" I recited the line my mother always used. While we didn't live close to other kids, a few neighbors had grandkids that visited and would ask to play if they saw us in the yard. My mother always sent them away.

"Do you have chores?" Gabriel asked.

I shook my head. Marie and I did split chores, but the house was usually pretty spotless. We were never outside our rooms so most of the house was never touched. Depending on my mom's mood now, Marie might be told to get on her knees in the kitchen for hours or something else. I shuddered, worried for her, too. I wondered what she was thinking to run outside like that. There was a possibility Marie thought Mom had been dead asleep. She was wrong. "I don't know what will happen to her."

Victor made a fist and then flopped back onto the bed. "I don't like this."

Kota and Nathan moved away from the window seat, but I remained, watching to see the boy disappear around the bend in the street. "It's her way of keeping control," I said softly. My face was radiating heat and I felt a tear in my eye and I blinked it back. I thought I had gotten used to the way my parents handled things. Keeping it in the dark was how I handled it.

Gabriel moved to sit on the bed near Victor's legs. He patted the floor below him with his hand, looking up at me. "Come here. Your hair is bugging me. Kota, do you have a brush?"

Kota leapt up and disappeared into his bathroom for a moment. He found a blue hair brush and tossed it over to Gabriel.

Gabriel caught it with one hand and curled his fingers at me. "Come on," he said.

I felt awkward, but did what I was told, moving to sit at his feet, leaning a little against the bed. I pulled the hair clip away, letting my hair fall in a wet clump against my neck.

"And what do you call this look? Wet shag?" His fingers fell over my hair, lightly tugging at the knots.

Victor toed at Gabriel's back to poke at him. "Leave her alone."

"Hey, I'm fixing it." He smoothed out my hair at the tips, starting with combing out the ends. "I'm going to detangle it, but we're going to wash it out and then dry it."

I shot a pleading look at Kota, feeling awkward. It was as if I was being told I didn't know how to handle my own body, like being told I was smelly and needed some deodorant. Kota didn't seem fazed by it.

"It's my fault," Nathan said. "I pushed her into the pool."

They all looked at him. I did, too. I hadn't expected him to talk about it. My blush continued on my face, now waiting to see if Kota or Victor appeared angry that I went swimming with Nathan instead of coming over. Why I felt that way, I wasn't sure.

Only they didn't look angry. They looked surprised. "What happened?" Kota asked.

Gabriel brushed out my hair while Nathan explained about how he found me in the tree and how he'd pushed me into the pool, all the way up until we were standing at Kota's door. He complimented my swimming. Again the warm, tender sensation washed over me. I appreciated how normal they were. We were talking and hanging around together. For the moment I was so glad they were forgetting about my problems. I tried not to look as excited as I was. I knew that Kota sitting on the floor a couple of feet away wasn't feeling his heart thudding or even thinking about the situation in the way I was. Touching, talking, laughing... So this is what happens when people got together?

I was envious of the years they must have spent together to be so comfortable with one another. Would I ever be so cozy with them? Would there ever be a day when I wasn't really conscious about the moment?

Gabriel patted my now smoothed strands of hair. Soft curls fell around my shoulders, still wet but now brushed.

"Your color is amazing," he said. "How is it so many different colors?"

I wasn't sure how to respond. "It's like a dirty blonde or something."

"Or something is right," he said. "There's a little red in there. Various shades of blonde. It's crazy." He urged me up by nudging me in the shoulder. "Let's go wash it. I want to blow dry it and see how it looks."

I again looked at Kota, who only smiled a little sympathetically at me. Nathan was smirking. I think he was enjoying this. I was feeling silly, but I stood up. Gabriel stood, grabbing my arm and pushing me toward Kota's bathroom.

He shut the bathroom door and we stood alone in the enclosed space. I felt my breath catch, not expecting this. Flashes of my imagination went through my head of things my mom would tell me about when boys got you alone. If being in Kota's room together with all of them wasn't bad enough, here I was in a locked room with one who wanted to play with my hair.

Gabriel went to Kota's shower and found a bottle of shampoo and conditioner. "These aren't ideal for you but it's what we have right now." He made a gesture to the sink and then patted me on the hip. "Let's get to work."

My cheeks radiated and I moved forward to face the sink.

Gabriel stood next to me and twisted the knobs, testing the temperature with his fingers. "Tell me when you think it's okay."

I reached in, waiting for the water to warm. When it did, I nodded to him.

"Get in there," he said.

I could hear voices from the other side of the door. I had a feeling it was about me, and I strained to hear over the sound of the rushing water.

When I ducked my head under the faucet, I couldn't hear the voices. Just Gabriel.

"You're going to our school, aren't you?" he asked, his

fingers combing through my hair again, rubbing along my scalp behind my ears and really working his fingers along the base of my head. The massaging motion relaxed me. He was good at this.

"Yes," I croaked, not sure what to say. I was feeling even shyer now that he'd seen such an intimate side of me and learned the awkwardness of my family. He just met me and he knew the worst things so far.

"We'll be in the same grade," he said. "Going to sign up for art class?"

I laughed. "I can't draw."

"Neither can I," he said. He moved behind me, I felt his hip meeting mine. Touching was impossible to get used to. I resisted the urge to leap away from him, though it was difficult. "I hear you just show up and play with paint. There's not much to it."

There was the fragrance of soap filling my nose and his fingers lathered up my hair with shampoo. "So you want an easy grade?" I asked.

"They don't offer the classes I want to take."

"What do you want to take?"

He finished rubbing the shampoo in and then pushed my head a little until I was further under the running water. He cupped his hand into the water to redirect the flow to run over the base of my neck. "I wouldn't mind learning bass. I already play guitar. There's one class at... um... another school." His fingers smoothed over the locks of my hair. I thought I felt him curling some of the strands but it was hard to tell.

His hesitation confused me. "Another school?"

"Just one of the private schools."

"Are you considering going to the private school next year?"

His hands moved away from my head and he was silent. I thought I might have said something wrong but I heard a bottle being squeezed and he was rubbing something between his hands. "Might."

"Is there a requirement to get in?"

He moved his fingers through my hair again, taking time to work the conditioner through every strand. "There's always a requirement for a private school, sweetie."

The endearment made my breath catch. People don't call other people sweetie up north, not unless they were sweethearts. I wondered if there was a hidden meaning, or if that was just how people talked here in the south, like I'd seen in movies.

"So it means you won't be going to my school if you go to the private one," I said softly.

"Maybe," he said. "Victor's so mean, isn't he? Did you see him kick me? I was trying to be nice and fix your hair and he's kicking me." Was he dodging the question, or was it obvious?

"He's not so bad," I said, thinking of the day before, how he had held my hand on the way out of the mall, and of the sheet music.

"No, he isn't bad. He's just a pain in the ass, sometimes." He finished the lather and then had me dunk my head into the water once more.

When I was finished and dripping into the sink, he found a towel in the tiny bathroom closet and held it out to me. I wrapped my hair into it while he dug around in the cabinet under the sink. He pulled out organized blue bins, reaching deeper inside for one near the back.

"So how do you know everyone?"

"Huh?" he asked, pulling an older model brown dryer out from under the sink.

I swallowed and tried to stage whisper. "I mean, how did you meet Kota? And Victor? When did you all become friends?"

He pushed the blue bins back underneath the sink and plugged in the dryer. He snapped his fingers and pointed at the closed toilet seat. When I was sitting, my head came up to his stomach. He flipped on the dryer and started combing his fingers through my hair. "I met them all in kindergarten," he said. "We went to the same elementary school. Everyone but Silas and North."

97

"Who's North?"

"Another one of the guys," he said. "There's me, Kota, Victor, Nathan, Silas, North and Luke."

"Who's Luke?"

"North's brother."

I blinked. Seven of them.

Gabriel reached for the hair brush on the counter and started smoothing out my hair. "You see, everyone except North and Silas grew up together. Silas didn't move here until maybe when we were ten. North came about a year later."

"Where was North?"

"He was living with his dad in Europe," he said, brushing my hair up against the air from the blower. "They live with their uncle now."

"Do they stop by here often?"

"You'll see them sometime," he said.

A silence grew between us as he focused on fixing my hair. With the way I was sitting, I couldn't see what he was doing to me. Mostly it felt like he was just drying it out, but he was doing a twist thing to add a little volume. It was more than I ever bothered to do.

There really was no reason for me to do more to it. I usually never saw anyone but my own family. Marie would trim my hair for me. She wasn't very good, but with my hair pulled back, no one noticed.

When he was done, he put down the dryer and the brush onto the counter top. He smoothed his fingers through my hair. "Your hair is soft. I was right about the color, too. It's chameleon."

"Huh?"

"Changes color depending on the light." He put the brush back in a drawer and then tossed the blow dryer under the sink. I wondered if Kota would be upset he didn't carefully put it back where he'd found it. Gabriel curled his finger to me. "Come here, step in front of me."

I stood in front of the sink and he stepped behind me. His eyes appeared over my head in the mirror and his fingers crept up to my scalp. He was playing with my hair, threading his fingers through the strands and combing out the locks to the tips of my hair. He tried curling a few strands around his fingers and then smoothed the hair back out again. "You're stunning," he said softly.

My cheeks heated and I could see myself blushing in the mirror, all the way to the tips of my ears.

"Don't be embarrassed," he said. "You can't be embarrassed by the truth. Look at that cute nose you have. You know what? It doesn't even matter when you blush. That's just nature's makeup. Heavy makeup looks like shit on a girl. You don't need it." He pursed his lips together and then brought his cheek to the side of my head so I could see his whole face next to mine in the mirror. He focused on my eyes by looking through the mirror. "I want to ask you something personal and I want you to be honest with me. You've never had a boyfriend, have you?"

The question caught me off guard. I shook my head and my mouth shaped into an 'o'.

"I didn't think so."

I made a face at him. "You think I'm naive?"

"Innocent," he corrected, his voice softer now. He curled a lock of my hair through his fingers. "I've been flirting with you this whole time and you haven't once told me to shut the fuck up or do that stupid thing girls do when they want another compliment."

I was beet red. Flirting? "Should I tell you to... to back off?"

His lips parted and he started to sing. *"Sang, heart on your sleeve. You watch out, I'm going to steal your heart."* The way he was singing was sweet and his voice flowed from his lips as smooth as water. It was clear he'd had some lessons. He stopped singing and waited as if expecting me to say something. When I didn't, he beamed. He turned and shooed me with his hands. "Let's get you out into the sunlight and see what your hair looks like."

I was blushing badly as I followed him back out into Kota's bedroom. My mind was whirling so fast that I felt like

I needed to stay behind and calm myself. It just shocked me that I hadn't recognized the things he was doing as flirting. Or was he teasing?

My hair did feel really good.

He padded back out into the bedroom and then side stepped, holding his hand out toward me in a presentation. "See guys, this is how hair should look."

Victor was still on the bed, fiddling with the medallion at his neck. Kota was at his computer, typing something in. Nathan was sitting in the window seat, punching something into his phone.

They all turned at the same time to look at me. Kota stopped typing and readjusted his glasses. Victor sat up, his mouth open. Nathan dropped his phone but caught it before it fell to the carpet.

"Did you change the color?" Kota asked.

"I didn't do shit," Gabriel said. "I washed it and then blow dried it out. That's all her."

"You just keep it tied back in that clip," Victor said. "That's why it looks different now."

I pulled a strand behind my ear. "It gets in the way when I'm busy." I wasn't sure if he heard me.

"Just wait until I get my scissors," Gabriel said. He reached back to me, running a finger through a lock of my hair close to my face. "I can give it some depth."

"I don't think I should," I said. "My parents will notice."

He made a face. "Your parents are a complication."

"We're working on that," Kota said.

I blinked at him. "I..." I swallowed.

Gabriel leaned in to me. "Just whisper it to me. I'll tell them."

I sighed and then whispered in his ear. He leaned in so closely that my lips touched his lobe. Even as I leaned away to avoid it, he kept himself close. He smelled like warmth, floral.

He repeated what I said, "She thinks we should keep like we're doing now. She's okay with escaping every morning and just not telling them where she's going."

"That's part of it, for now," Kota said. He stood up, moving to sit on the carpet again. I moved over to sit next to him. This time Victor got up and sat on the floor next to me. The others joined us. "I made a promise to you, didn't I? I just think we need to figure out a way to reach you. We probably also should slowly start just showing up. I mean, maybe your mom would get used to us."

My eyes widened and I shook my head. "No. We can't." They still didn't quite understand, but I didn't want to worry them anymore. The swallowing vinegar was bad enough but who knew what else she would do to me if she knew for sure boys were talking to me? Would she fulfill her promise about the bleach?

He nodded, rubbing fingers at his chin. "Maybe we should start with a girl. There's Danielle who lives up the street. We could ask her to go over."

Nathan rolled his eyes, looking away. "Is she going to want to?"

"She's not that bad."

"Unless you try to talk to her," Gabriel said.

"Or sit next to her on the bus," Nathan said.

"Or walk by her in school," Victor added.

"She's who we have to work with," Kota pointed out. "Or we could try Jessica. But she's young, so I don't know how that would work." He turned back to me. "In the meantime, I was wondering if you'd allow us to give you a cell phone to use."

My head tilted backward a little and I stammered. "M... me?"

"I think it'll be the best way to check in with you and make plans if we're going to make any. It'll be the best way to communicate."

I rubbed a palm over my head. "I don't know. You guys are going through a lot of trouble for me already. You still hardly know me."

"It's a cell phone, not a marriage proposal," Victor said. His strong, lean hands smoothed a wrinkle on his jeans.

"It costs money," I said. "I don't really have a way to pay for it."

"That's not something you need to worry about," Victor said. He locked his fire eyes on me.

"We'll find an inexpensive one at the convenience store," Kota said. "Nothing fancy. It'll allow for phone calls and text messages."

I glanced at the carpet, still feeling uncomfortable. How strange it felt that they were including me into this circle. Now they were pulling together to get a cell phone for me. Guilt weighed on me that they even thought to spend any amount of money on someone like me. As I looked at all of them, it seemed as if this decision had already been made. They were just waiting to tell me. "I'll have to be careful," I said. "If my parents ever found it, I don't know what they would do."

"Do you have a place to hide it?" Nathan asked, raising an eyebrow.

"Maybe. There's an attic door in my room," I said, pushing a finger to my lower lip.

"Why not just under your pillow?" Gabriel asked.

"Someone will find it," I said. Unless I stayed right there in my room, it's easy enough to unlock the door and poke around. My mother could easily search my room, if she wanted and Marie often did anyway. A phone was the last thing I wanted any of them to find.

"You do it the best you can," Kota said. He turned to Victor. "Can you go find one?"

Victor nodded and stood up.

"Get her a pretty one," Gabriel said. He smiled wide and turned to me. "If you're going to get a new phone, you'll need a good one. What's your favorite color?"

I blushed as the attention was diverted to me again. Should I be honest or say something I thought was cool? "Pink," I said, trying to be honest.

Gabriel's blue eyes brightened. "Yeah. Good choice. Get her a pink one."

Victor smirked. "One pink cell phone."

"Try to get her one that's inconspicuous," Kota added.

"One inconspicuous pink phone."

"And get her a sturdy one," Nathan said. "She might drop it. You know how accident prone she is" He grinned at me.

Victor shifted on his feet, looking annoyed. "One inconspicuous, sturdy, pink cell phone. Do I need to glue sequins to it and include an antenna array?"

"Do they have those?" Gabriel asked, blinking at him.

Victor shot him a look. "I'll be right back." He fished out his keys and headed to the stairs, storming down them and closing the door with a bang.

After he left, Kota adjusted his glasses again. "Well, that's taken care of."

"I don't know," I whispered.

Kota pointed a forefinger at me. "Sang, look at me."

I focused on him. His smile and his eyes were so warm that it was hard to keep looking at him. Why did it feel he could read my own thoughts in my head? I wanted to hide my face.

"We're friends, right?"

I blushed. Were we? It was the very thing I wanted to know from him. Are we still friends even after all of this? "Yes," I said, hopeful it was the right answer.

"Friends help each other. Stop worrying, okay? We'll take care of it."

I twisted my lips, trying to come up with a reason to stop it, but nothing seemed to be the right thing to say. I felt helpless, moving along with a plan they had already plotted.

Nathan got up on his knees on the floor. "I'm hungry. I'm going to go steal a sandwich, Kota."

"There's a couple of frozen ones in the freezer," Kota suggested. "Heat it up in the microwave for a minute."

Nathan pointed a finger at me. "Do you want one? I'll bring you up one. I know you haven't eaten yet."

I'd forgotten about that. I glanced at Kota, unsure if I should.

"It's perfectly fine," Kota said.

Nathan disappeared down the stairs.

"Now," Kota began after he left. "We should probably talk about school and your classes."

"Classes?" Why were we talking about this? I looked at Gabriel, but he was unreadable. Should we worry about this now? It did relax me, though, that they had seemed to move on from talking about what happened with my mother. I felt so terrible already, like I was causing them problems being around. It amazed me they were bothering. If they were willing to put up with me, I would do my best not to drag them down.

Kota nodded. "Registration is the day after tomorrow. Your parents will be taking you?"

I nodded. "My dad."

Gabriel scooted over next to me. "Art class, right?"

I smiled at him. "If they don't mind stick figures," I whispered.

Kota got up to move to his desk and opened a drawer. He pulled out an envelope and brought it over. "This is the list of classes that will be available."

He opened it to reveal several printed out pages. Some of the classes were highlighted in various colors.

"There's the obvious," he said. "English, geometry and a history class. Any particular interests there?"

I checked over the list. "What's AP?"

"The more advanced classes."

"The English one says they read novels?"

The corner of his mouth worked up into a smile. "I think it'll be a pretty fast paced class. You'd have to read the required pages every day."

"That's not a problem," I said. "Better than the text books." I looked back at the papers he'd given me, but I could sense Gabriel and Kota exchanging looks. Was I being stupid? "Is the only Asian history class an AP class?" My voice failed with the last word, and I swallowed. Talking was taking a toll on my throat, and it felt itchy. I wanted to cough but I didn't want to worry them.

"I think that's for seniors. There's prerequisites before

you can take it."

"How about world history?" Gabriel asked.

"I guess so."

Kota knelt next to me. His body was close to mine as he looked over my shoulder and I could feel his warmth and caught his spice scent. He seemed so focused that it didn't appear to bother him. "There's not too many class varieties, unfortunately. You'd be able to take the AP geometry without getting too bogged down."

I smirked. "I want to take the AP geometry?"

"It's the same numbers; they just go at slightly different learning speeds. Besides, you'll share the class with Nathan or someone else most likely. I can help if you need it."

"What classes are you taking?"

He smiled. "Particle physics and the AP calculus, although I don't really need it. A refresher is always nice. They don't have anything better. I'll probably take that AP English."

"No advanced particle English?" I asked.

Gabriel rocked back with his hand on his chest and laughed. "If there was, he'd take it."

"What's so funny?" Nathan asked, coming up the stairs. He had two sandwiches wrapped in paper towels in his hands, and a bottle of water under his arm. He handed me one of the sandwiches. "I hope you like chicken."

I nodded, taking the bottle of water from him, too. He dropped himself into the window seat and opened a grilled chicken sandwich on a seeded bun.

"We're figuring out what classes Sang wants to take," Kota said. "We've got three down. We need three more."

"There's the gym glass we have to do," Nathan said. He came across the room, reaching for the open bottle of water in my hand. He took a chug of water, swallowing and handing it back to me before he continued. "Might as well take it now."

"I think they separate the boys and girls for that," Gabriel said.

"Yeah, into groups, but we're all mixed together in that

one gym at the same time. Like the boys get one half and the girls get the other." Nathan took a bite of sandwich, chewing and then talked with food in his mouth. "I mean, if any one of us has the same class, we're across the room."

"Do I need to be in everyone's same class?" I asked. The fresh water gave me a little voice back, just enough to do a notch above a stage whisper. I picked a piece of the bread off of my sandwich and ate it.

"There's just a strong likelihood a lot of us will be paired up," Kota said. "There's a limited variety of classes and we're mostly all taking the same courses."

I shrugged. So their goal with school was getting into as many of the same classes as possible. If that was the case, why was Kota taking separate classes? I supposed studying together would be nice. However, there was more to this. Gabriel and Nathan acted as if this was normal. This was how they functioned together. Kota took the lead and everyone worked on it. Did other students try to take all the same classes so they would most likely get paired up together?

I was going to take another bite of my sandwich, when Gabriel reached over and took my wrist. He looked right at me, never wavering his gaze, and then brought the sandwich to his face, with me holding it still, and took a small bite.

"Get your own sandwich," Nathan said, tossing a crumpled up paper towel at him.

Gabriel dodged the paper. "I just wanted a taste."

I giggled, but I caught the look in Gabriel's eye. I wondered if this was flirting. Was I supposed to say something?

Kota had a piece of paper in his hand, writing down notes. He slowly slid the glasses on his nose up with his forefinger. "That's four classes," Kota said. "Two more."

"Science," Gabriel said. "Chemistry."

"I haven't taken biology yet," I said. "Last year at my old school, the class was filled. I'd need the biology since it's a prerequisite."

"She can take the typing class," Nathan said.

"You make it sound like she's going to be a secretary," Gabriel said. "Maybe she should take a class in shorthand, too."

"That's not what I meant," Nathan said. "Don't put words in my mouth. I was just saying it's an easy class. Besides, there's no homework and it'll be an easy grade to boost her GPA early. Especially if you're going to stick her into a couple of AP classes right off."

"Three," I said. "There's an AP biology." All of them looked at me. My cheeks heated up again. Did I say something silly? "Science is science. It's not like the frog's gut chart changes depending on the class you take."

They all laughed.

The sound of a car pulling up distracted us.

"It must be Victor with the phone," Kota said.

Victor was up the stairs in a few minutes. He held a bag in his hands. His cheeks looked a little flushed, like he had been in a hurry. He plopped down onto the floor next to me with the package. "I didn't see a pink one," he said. "But there was a pink case. It'll protect the phone."

I smiled shyly, unsure what to say. Thinking of a phone was one thing, but looking at the new bag in his hands, I felt my fingers trembling. "Thank you," I said softly, unsure how to argue about having it now if he'd already gone through the trouble to get it.

He took it out of the bag and then pulled the box apart. It was the latest iPhone, identical to the one he had.

"I thought I said just simple calling and texting," Kota said. "What happened to inconspicuous?"

"It does text," Victor said, his face tightening. "It also takes pictures and downloads apps. Sue me." He handed me the phone.

The touch screen was super clean and the app dashboard was bare, except for Angry Birds.

"I filled in a few essentials on there," Victor said. "I also put in everyone's phone number."

It took me a moment to figure out which button held the phone numbers. I thumbed through the contacts page.

"Including North and Luke?"

"You would have gotten those eventually, anyway," Kota said.

"Who's Blackbourne?"

Victor's eyes went wide. I caught out of the corner of my eye the other boys looking directly at him and looking panicked. "Oh, sorry. Here, let me see that."

He took the phone from me and pushed buttons until it was deleted.

"Sorry," he said. "Just an old teacher. I don't know how I transferred that one."

He seemed to play it off, but I caught the look Nathan and the others exchanged. It was very slight, but it was obvious this was more information I wasn't really supposed to see.

What was going on with these guys?

When I left Kota's house that afternoon, I walked around the street and then took a path through the woods to find myself in my back yard. It was a long route but I really didn't want anyone to see me leaving from Kota's house.

Before I left, Kota had me send a text to everyone so they could add me to their phones, including North and Luke. North was the only one who sent a message back right away.

North: "Ok."

I had the phone tucked into the cup of my bra. It was the best way to hide it for now. If I just tried to keep it in my pocket, I was afraid it would slip, or my mom would notice the bulge.

I had to pull my hair back, too. Gabriel was disappointed, but I told him if I came home with it down, it'd draw unneeded attention. My mother would already be angry over Marie with the boy from up the road. As it was, I'd have to convince her I was only walking in the woods if she asked.

When I got into the house, I made a dash up the stairwell. The rear stairwell was a lifesaver, enabling me to leave the house unnoticed. It came out by the laundry room which had the side door to the garage.

Upstairs, I knocked on Marie's door to check on her.

Marie answered, her long brown hair hanging behind her shoulders. Her nose and chin were sharp, her brown eyes smaller than mine. She was taller, too, by at least a foot. Her hips were wider. For sisters, we didn't look a lot alike. "What?" she whined.

"What happened earlier?" I croaked. Marie didn't look upset and she could talk so it must not have been too bad this time.

"Mom was looking for you," she said, stepping out of the way. Her room had various piles of clothes on the floor and notebooks across her bed.

"I know," I said, even though I didn't. "I'm going to take my shoes off and then I'll go get yelled at."

I didn't have to explain it. She knew exactly what I meant. Seeing our mother usually involved yelling and often a punishment. It was painful to kneel on the floor for hours with shoes on.

I crossed the hallway and used a push pin tucked into the wall to unlock my door and get in to my room. Marie knew how to unlock my door and knew where I hid the pushpin. For me, it was just a small deterrent. It allowed me time to hear someone coming if I was inside. No one would bother knocking and I couldn't force them to stay out.

When I was inside, I relocked the door before pulling the cell phone out of my bra. I was tempted to play with it, but instead went for the attic space door. I reached in and found an opening between the wood of the wall and the insulation. I tucked the phone between them. I had the cord in my front pocket and I put that in the attic with it. On a final thought, I turned up the stereo music a little to detract from any noise the phone could make. I had been careful to turn that off when I got it, but I still worried it would vibrate or beep or something.

"Sang!" I heard my mother calling. She must have heard when I turned up the volume on the radio. "Come down here!"

I sighed, wishing I was still back at Kota's.

Downstairs, I entered my mother's bedroom. Her inner sanctum. Her wiry hair looked disheveled, like it hadn't been brushed in days. She sat with her back against the headboard, frowning at me. "Where have you been?"

"In the shed."

"All day?"

I nodded. "I was looking to see if I had any more clothes for school in the boxes we haven't unpacked yet," I strained to be heard from across the room so I wouldn't have to come closer. I knew what was coming and was ready.

"You shouldn't do that," she said. "I will go through it when I'm ready to. I don't want you going through it."

"Oh," I said, pretending to not understand. A little trouble would stop her from prodding further, I hoped. "Sorry," I added.

"Some... man," she spat out the word, "came here today to play basketball with Marie."

Derrick, I thought. For some reason I thought he was my age and didn't appear to be someone to be worried about. I tried to look confused. "Who was it?"

"I don't remember his name. He said he went to your school."

I nodded, pretending to think. "Well, there's bound to be a kid or two around the block."

"How would you know?" she asked, digging at my story. "How did he know there were kids here? I don't think you should be walking around in the yard anymore. They might come over again."

"But I haven't run into anyone."

She mumbled something to herself, licking at her cracked lips. "I don't want you hanging around with men."

"I haven't met anyone," I repeated.

She pressed her lips together tightly. She had no proof

otherwise, I knew. Depending on her mood, it could be bad or good. "Is your room clean?" she asked. A sharp odor hit my nose from the room, like rubbing alcohol.

"Almost," I said. It was like playing a game. If I gave the right answer, I got the answer I wanted. Right now, if she stuck me in my room it didn't matter. It was where I wanted to be anyway.

"Well, go to your room. Don't come out until it's spotless."

"Okay," I said and I tried to go to the door.

"I mean it," she said, her voice commanding that I stay and hear her out on her instructions. "I want the trash put into a trash bag."

"Okay."

"And the clothes off the floor and hung up."

"Right."

"And I want to hear the vacuum running."

"I'll get on it now," I said, edging toward the door. I coughed. She didn't say anything about my throat or ask about it. I wondered if she even remembered what she'd done.

It was still another ten minutes before I got out of her room as she lectured me on how to clean. I was elated. I had all night to myself with a good excuse. I'd been grounded to my room until it was clean. I could be fairly undisturbed for a while. It was the punishment I could deal with happily.

I rushed up the stairs and then locked my door behind me. My room didn't have trash or clothes on the ground. The floor was bare. I smiled to myself and shook my head. If she came up to check, there was nothing for her to say about it. There was hardly a thing in my room to mess it up with.

I went to the attic door and pulled out the cell phone.

If someone wanted to unlock the door and look in, I'd have about a split second to listen to the rattle of the handle before it opened. I cuddled up over near the window. I sat on the trunk, looking out to check Kota's house. Victor's car was still there, but he'd said he was going to stick around for dinner. Victor and Kota and Gabriel had a movie they wanted

111

to watch. Nathan had gone home. He claimed he had a few chores to do around the house.

I grabbed a book from the shelf and sprawled out on the floor next to my trunk. If someone rattled the door, I could drop the phone behind the trunk and quickly pick up the book to look like I had been reading.

I checked the messages, but no one had sent me anything. I hovered my fingers over the displayed keyboard, wondering what I could do. And who would I text? I didn't know what to say to anyone.

To pass the time and to keep myself busy, I focused on the Angry Birds app.

♥♥♥

I got tired of Angry Birds quickly. I spent a lot of time on the floor, just looking up at the ceiling and listening to the music from my stereo. The sun started to go down. I checked outside; Victor's car was gone from Kota's driveway, so he was already home or on his way.

I had the phone on my stomach when it started to vibrate. It spooked me and I shivered. The phone slid down to the floor and flopped over. I sat up quickly, so fast, it made me dizzy, and turned on the screen.

Silas: "Good."

He was responding to the message I had sent earlier about getting this new phone. I pondered what I would send him next, then quickly typed in:

Sang: "How was practice?"
Silas: "Long. I'm tired."

Should I stop texting? I wondered. He probably wanted to rest and didn't want me bugging him.

The phone rattled in my hands.

Silas: "What are you doing?"

I looked nervously around the room. *What am I doing? I'm obsessively hanging on to this phone and attempting to sound cool to you so you'll like me.*

Before I could answer, the phone vibrated again. Silas was calling.

My heart dropped in my chest. I wasn't sure if I could get away with answering it. I wouldn't hear Marie or anyone coming. And I couldn't talk! What could I do?

In my panic, I hit the button. I couldn't just not answer.

"Hello?" I said softly into the receiver.

"I'm not good at texting," Silas's deep voice floated to my ear. Just hearing his low, masculine tones made my insides flip. "I've got rhino fingers."

I chuckled. "You were doing okay," I whispered, my eyes darting around my room. Could I slip into the attic space? My closet?

"This is easier," he said. "So what are you doing?"

I carefully held the phone to my ear with my shoulder and then unlocked the window. "Not a lot. I was reading."

"Did you read all day?"

I held the phone to my chest and heaved a foot out onto the rooftop. The wind was blowing softly outside, but it was the safest place to be nearby and not get caught. I brought the phone back to my ear, using my shoulder again to hold it as I eased myself out. "I went swimming with Nathan, too. And I met Gabriel."

"Did he mess with your hair?"

I laughed. "How'd you know?" I put my butt down on the rooftop, scooting myself until I was sitting next to the window rather than in front of it. If someone tried to get into my room, I might not hear them from outside but if I tucked myself out of the way, the person wouldn't see me out there. It would just look like my window was open. Hopefully no one would be interested in looking outside.

"I think he's done everyone's since I've known him," he said. "I haven't paid for a haircut since I came here."

"You moved here when you were little, right?"

The phone vibrated in my hand and there was a beep. I moved it away from my head. It said there was a message coming in. I felt my heart beating wildly with the desire to check it out but I didn't know the buttons to push to look at it without hanging up on Silas.

As it was, since I was distracted, I missed half of his answer. I put the phone to my ear again just as he was saying, "-- it's different here, but I guess I'll manage."

"I'll have to find a way to manage, too, I guess."

He laughed. "Not so bad right now, is it?"

Another vibration, another beep. This time I caught the name. It was from Kota. I still didn't know what to do, so I ignored it again.

"I think it's pretty nice here. I mean I met you and the others. You guys are cool," I croaked. Lame! I put my hand to my cheek, feeling it warming. I didn't know how to talk to people.

He was quiet for a moment. "Do you think we can hang out tomorrow?"

Another vibrate, another beep. Kota.

"I suppose so. I don't know how to... um," I wasn't sure the words to say and Kota's messages were distracting me so badly, I couldn't think.

"I've got a car. I probably need to meet you at Kota's, right?"

"Yeah, probably," I squeaked as I whispered.

Pause. Did he hear what I said? "Is your voice okay?"

I swallowed, trying my best. "I'm fine."

"I'll have to do stuff in the morning but I can swing by later in the afternoon."

"Perfect." Was this him asking for just us or was he coming over to hang out with me and Kota? He was asking me personally, right? I didn't know how to take the question.

The phone vibrated and started beeping, Kota was calling.

"What's that noise?"

"Kota's calling," I said. "I don't really know how to switch over the line..."

"It's okay," Silas said. "Go ahead and answer him. I'll talk to you later."

I wasn't sure, but he sounded disappointed in having to go so soon. "Okay, bye."

"Bye."

I pushed the big green button on the phone to answer Kota's call.

"Hel--?"

"Get off the roof, Sang!"

His tone was stressed. Was he mad at me? "Kota, I..."

"Hide the phone in your pocket and go outside behind your shed. Go now." He hung up.

I felt my legs shaking underneath me when I tried to stand up. Kota was scaring the bejeezus out of me.

I scrambled through the window. I tried to shut it but it got stuck halfway down and I left it. I tucked the phone back into the cup of my bra. I stopped to double check that everything looked normal, and then went for the door.

The house was quiet. I slipped down the hallway, trying not to make a sound as I tiptoed down the back stairwell and out into the garage.

I jogged out into the open driveway, down to the end of it to the shed. I circled around, the grass warm under my bare feet. The back of the shed had a concrete patio and an overhang. It was kind of like a third porch. I think it was meant for a place to stick a barbecue pit or maybe even a car because there looked like an oil slick on one side. It wouldn't allow much protection if Marie left the house to come look for me, but it did block me from the windows and I was out of voice distance, in case someone could actually hear me from my bedroom.

The phone started to shake in my hands. Kota was calling and I tapped the green button.

"What were you doing on the roof?" he demanded, his voice intense.

"I wasn't sure if I should answer the phone in the house."

He breathed out into the phone, causing it to crackle with noise. "I thought you were going to fall off. You've gotten into enough trouble this week without needing to go to the hospital."

"It's okay," I said. "That area over the roof of the porch is pretty flat. Besides, the drop isn't that far."

"It could break your neck," he said.

"I've been trained on how to fall," I insisted.

He paused. "What do you mean?"

"Back in elementary school, in gym class. They taught us to fall from a tall distance."

"How?"

"Depends on the distance," I said. "If it's pretty far, there's this thing where you tuck and roll to keep going on that momentum so you don't break your hands and knees."

He laughed, the power in his voice slipped away, becoming friendly. "And they were teaching you this in elementary school?"

"I think they might not do it anymore. After a week of training, some of us were out on the school jungle gym taking turns *practicing* falling. We got caught pretty quickly and we got reprimanded about it. I may or may not have been involved."

He laughed again. "You are a trouble maker. But that's no excuse. Don't climb out on the roof."

"What if there's a fire?"

"Unless there's a fire."

"What if there's a robber with a gun?"

"Sang."

"Or a zombie?" I giggled.

"You don't run from zombies. You shoot them in the head."

"I don't have a gun."

"I'm not buying you a gun."

I laughed this time and he did too. "Oh, Silas called and said he might come over tomorrow afternoon." I hoped he meant to hang out with Kota and the others. Going solo was too nerve-wracking to think about.

"That's good. I heard North and Luke were coming, too. They had something they wanted to tell us."

There was a beep from the phone and I checked it. It was from Luke.

"Luke's sending me a message right now."

"Well you should go answer him," Kota said. "Just stay off your roof, okay? I'll tell everyone to text you to call them and you will do it as soon as you can. No surprise calls."

I agreed and hung up. Still, the conversation bugged me. He had been watching me from his window? Now he was telling everyone the best way to communicate with me. Leader of the group. What kind of group was this?

$\mathcal{L}$UKE

hen I got back to my bedroom without anyone noticing, I was relieved. I huddled back near the window and checked the message from Luke.

Luke: "Hi."

I laughed a little, giddy. I had boys texting me. It was like something out of a movie I'd seen. How stupid was I to get excited over a text?

Sang: "Hello."

I tried to suppress my excitement. I really wanted to go for a walk to release some of this energy, but now that I was back in the house again, I didn't want to go through the effort to sneak out. This phone was much more fun than I'd anticipated. I had friends calling me! It was easier to pretend I was normal this way.

The phone buzzed in my hand.

Luke: "I'm Lucian but everyone calls me Luke. You're Sang, right? Where did you move from?"
Sang: "I'm from up north. The south is different."
Luke: "It's warmer, but it's probably the same."
Sang: "There's also palm trees."
Luke: "LOL"

The Academy - Introductions

Sang: "Are you coming over tomorrow? Kota mentioned it."
Luke: "Yeah. In the morning, I think."
Sang: "What's the big announcement?"
Luke: "Promise not to tell?"

Would I tell? Promise? Would he trust me? He hadn't even met me yet.

Sang: "I promise."
Luke: "Pinkie swear?"
Sang: "How can I pinkie swear if I'm not there to shake your pinkie?"

It was two minutes before I got another message. This time it was a picture message. There was a male hand in the shot, the pinkie lifted up, partially curled.

I thought it was funny. It took me a minute to figure out how the camera worked and to take a photo but I returned one of my pinkie in the same position.

Luke: "Your hands are small."
Sang: "How can you tell?"
Luke: "There's a book in the shot. Is that Grimm's Fairy Tales?"

I hadn't even looked at what I put nearby. It was a Grimm book.

Sang: "Yes."
Luke: "Which one's your favorite?"

My mind had gone blank. I flipped through the pages to look for a title that I recognized.

Sang: "I like The Princess in Disguise. So what's your big news?"
Luke: "We're buying the church on your block."
Sang: "What? Why?"

Before I got a text back, I heard a rattling at my door. I dropped the phone behind the trunk against the wall and picked up the book. I heard it clunk and I stressed, worried I might have broken it. What would Victor think if I broke the brand new phone he bought for me?

The door swung wide open. My older sister Marie poked her head in. Her dark eyes narrowed in on me.

"Mom wants you to come down for din-nur," she cooed.

"Ugh," I said. "What is it?"

"Beef stew."

We'd had canned beef stew three times that week already. Most of the time, my mother didn't care if we showed up, but when she was in a particularly annoyed mood, she tried giving us orders on when to eat, when to sleep and so on. "I don't really want any," my voice cracking as I spoke.

"She'll just yell for you in a minute, anyway."

I grumbled. She was right. "Hang on, let me close this window." It was still open, and I was grateful. It gave me an excuse to stay there for a few minutes. Marie disappeared, not bothering to shut the door. I heard her thud down the stairs.

I did close the window but I checked the phone quickly before tucking it away in the attic.

Luke: "We're opening a diner."

That night, I was still awake at midnight when I got the last text from Victor.

Victor: "I'll let you go to sleep."

I was grateful for it. My thumbs tingled. Luke had told me about his uncle who wanted to open up a restaurant, so they were going to do a diner and use the church building. He sounded excited about it, but soon had to go to eat dinner, too. Gabriel wanted to talk about what I was going to wear to registration and was telling me about the school building being a drab box with windows. Victor asked when my birthday was.

Sang: "October."
Victor: "Mine's in January."

The next morning, I was out the door the moment my dad took off to go to work. I couldn't sleep at all the night before, but I was grateful, since not sleeping meant there weren't any nightmares. I stole down to the garage, taking the plug for the phone. I charged it from the inside of the shed where I was shielded from view. It took only fifteen minutes. When it was filled, I hid the plug and pocketed the phone, heading for the woods again.

I should have been tired since I hadn't slept, but the air was so fresh and I felt really good. I was only wearing sandals this time, with a short green cotton skirt and a thin yellow hoodie with three-quarter sleeves and a front pocket. I brushed my hair out and pulled it up into a neater twist with my clip, leaving two locks on either side of my face, tucked behind my ears. I thought it framed my face better. I giggled at myself that morning in the bathroom for being concerned with my looks now. I always thought other girls at school were silly to spend so much time fixing their hair and makeup for school classes. A week ago, I wouldn't have cared how I looked.

I tested my voice as I walked. Since I was able to rest it, I could speak softly, but it started to crack if I talked at a normal level. I was hopeful by the time Silas came around, it would be even better. I didn't want him wondering what happened.

I had the phone tucked into my hoodie pocket as I walked. I fiddled with it in my hands as I took the shortcut through the woods. When Luke talked about his plans to turn the church into a diner, I wanted to check it out before it all changed.

If it wasn't for the large cross over the door, the

building might have looked like any old utility building. The windows were maybe a couple of feet long and narrow along the side. The large white double front doors were plain, clean cut. The metal siding was a bland beige. Still, the building looked clean. There was a large blue jungle gym and a swing set nearby. The grass around it was a little high. I climbed onto the landing of the gym set, sitting on it and swinging my feet off of the edge as I tried to picture the place as a diner. The parking lot was gravel, but still very usable. The small attempt at a border garden around the front had a few stick trees and dead bushes. It would take a lot of work to make it look attractive.

I felt the phone in my pocket vibrating and it tickled. Who was up this early?

Luke: "What's your favorite breakfast?"

I smiled to myself, thinking about the answer. It was silly but it wasn't embarrassing. Would he think I was childish?

Sang: "Chocolate chip pancakes."

"With syrup?" a voice asked behind me.

Startled, I twisted myself, nearly falling off the ledge and I reached out to the pole support to hold myself up. On the ground behind me was a guy with blond hair so long it almost touched his shoulders. Most of it was pulled back into a loose ponytail behind his head. Several locks hung around his ears and in his face. He was wearing dark blue Levi jeans, black flip flops and a white button up shirt with the collar looking rumpled. The top three buttons were undone, so I could see halfway down his chest through the opening. The bottom button was undone as well. I wondered why he bothered with the shirt at all. His skin was only a smidgen darker than my own. His eyes were brown, striking against his light hair and features. He had high cheekbones and a strong chin. Of all the guys I had met so far, if I had to pick out which one would be the most popular with girls, he would have beaten them all by miles. I could easily imagine him being a model.

I knew my mouth was hanging open and I quickly closed it, trying to process his question. Did I hear him right? I swallowed to make sure my voice would work. "Luke?"

He put his hand to his waist and made the smallest of bows, a wide smile on his face. "In the flesh." He stood up and reached for a rung on the monkey bars, picking up his feet to hang from it. I could see his belly button and the defined muscles of his abdomen as his shirt rode up his body. He wasn't as cut as Nathan, but he was clearly strong. "What do you think? Can you see it as a diner?" he asked.

I looked toward the church, tilting my head. "I think it depends on what the inside looks like."

"Not judging the book by the cover, huh?" he smiled and then crossed the monkey bars hand over hand, swinging his body as he did, until he could put his feet on the platform where I sat. "We have to get rid of the playground, though," he said. "Insurance would kill us if we kept it."

"That's a shame," I said. "Would have been a good way to bring in parents with kids."

"I know," he said. "It's going on fall now but I thought about setting up a patio up front. Improving the size of the garden a little, maybe?"

The yard of the church was at least an acre. It sat right on the corner where the highway met the residential road. The neighborhood homes were tucked behind a row of evergreen trees, so there was some separation and the neighbors probably wouldn't notice or hear the traffic to the diner. The would-be diner had easy access to a fairly busy road and no competition within miles. "What made you guys want to start a diner?"

"It's what my uncle wants to do," he said. He leaned back against a pole, looking at me with those dark eyes. They were playful, like he wanted to laugh, and he was just waiting for the joke. "He was working with a partner and the partner is kicking him out. So he's starting his own place."

"That's too bad," I said. He looked confused. "I mean it's too bad that his partner wanted to split up. Were they friends?"

"I think when they started," he said. He moved away from the post and leaned toward me. "So you want to see it?"

I tilted my head at him, an eyebrow going up. "The inside?" I smiled. Exploring? Of course. "Yes."

He jumped down from the platform. The scent of something sweet came from him as he passed me. He moved around in front of me and held up his arms until his hands were on the outside of my thighs. From where I was sitting, I could see the muscle tone in his arm flexing. His eyes focused directly into mine.

"Let's go."

It was as if it were as natural as breathing, which surprised me later when I thought about it. I reached out and he moved his shoulders so I could balance myself and hop down. He had me by the hips and lowered me gently to the ground. He held on to me when I started to step back as if he was worried I had stumbled.

The moment I was stable, he let go of me and turned to walk toward the church, pulling keys from his pocket. It was like he never gave any thought to the moment between us that felt so intimate to me. My family never hugged each other. I barely remembered the last time I even touched hands with one of them. He helped me down from the gym as if it were just the thing to do. Was it normal? So many of the boys had touched me this week, that I was feeling a crazy sense of loneliness when they let go.

I followed on his heels toward the front door, my eyes going up to the cross. It felt like it should almost be sacred, but would it feel differently once it was converted?

Luke fit the key into the door lock and then held it open for me. I stepped inside, smelling the heavy dust and stale air. The hallway in front of us was in shadow.

He closed the door and moved forward. At a certain point in the hallway, it started getting super dark. I was trying to reach out with one hand for a wall to help guide me but something touched my hand and I jumped.

"Here," Luke said and he reached for my hand again. "Stay behind me. I'm sorry; I don't know where the light switch is. It didn't seem that dark down here when we started."

I sucked in a breath and followed behind him. His hand was warm, his fingers interlocking with mine. My heart fluttered. He was just helping, I told myself. Normal people do this when necessary. I needed to get used to it.

Near the end of the hallway, a window provided a little more light. There was a wide, double door to our right. He let go of my hand to open it.

The inside was pitch black.

"Hold the door open," Luke said. "I'll find the switch."

I stood by the door as Luke disappeared into the darkness. Minutes passed. I was worried he might fall or something might happen to him. How could I find him in the dark?

Electricity crackled above my head and the lights flickered on. There were two sets of chandeliers; a couple of the bulbs were missing but it mostly worked. We were in the chapel, though the pews were gone and there were a couple of faded green hymnals stacked along the walls. There was a platform on the far end, a podium in front with a cross on it. The carpet was a dull brown, the walls a yellowed off-white.

Luke was standing on the platform near the back wall. He walked toward the front of it, looking around the room and his hands slid into his pockets. "Well? What do you think?"

I swept my eyes across the room, trying to imagine what it would look like as a diner. "There's a lot of space for tables," I offered. Still, it was a vast, empty space that could be used for anything.

"And this stage could be used for bands on some nights." Luke stomped on the wood of the platform. "It feels solid."

I tiptoed through the room. There was a slight chill in the air. At least the air conditioning unit worked. I crossed my arms over my chest and rubbed at goose bumps. There were exposed beams. I could imagine the lights all working, a cozy setting with booths for customers. I wondered where the kitchen was.

Luke materialized behind me, standing close with his chest warming my back. I froze. I felt his lips near my ear. "Do you see it?" he whispered.

I swallowed, nervous. I wasn't sure if I could turn around and look at him. I nodded. "It just needs the right tables."

"And the door over there could be the official entrance," he said, moving to my side to stand next to me and pointing. "And the other, the entryway to the kitchen. We'll have to get rid of the podium."

"You should keep it," I said. "You could paint it and attach it to something so you could roll it in when you want to. You could rent the place out for meetings."

His eyes popped open wide. "I hadn't even thought about that."

"And I like the garden and outside dining idea," I said.

"There could be a bar over there," he motioned with his hand. "A big one."

"And a case for pies and baked things you'd sell on the side," I added.

"And a jukebox."

"With vases of flowers on the tables."

His breath caught and his shimmering eyes sought out mine. "What's your favorite flower?"

I smiled. "I like roses. Chrysler Imperial."

He grinned, showing his perfect white teeth. "We'll have a rose garden out front. We'll be able to put roses out on the tables for most of the year."

I laughed, waving my hand in the air. "What about when the roses die off in the winter?"

His mouth twisted and he turned partially away from me, shifting on his feet. "We'll light candles. Rose scented ones."

My heart warmed. His imagination was intoxicating. I

could see everything he had suggested. Before my eyes, the dullness of the church washed away, and all I could see was a crowded diner. Luke would wear a serving apron and would hold a tray steaming with fresh food. I even entertained the idea of running the counter, serving coffee and helping people with their purchases. I could see Kota and Nathan as customers, Victor playing piano on stage, and Gabriel or maybe Silas helping in the kitchen.

I had turned to look at the large empty space again. I felt Luke next to me. His fingertips brushed at the top of my hand. It was so unexpected that I pulled my hand away before I had a chance to stop myself.

"You see it, don't you?" he asked. There was a gleam in his eyes, as if he needed me to believe in this as much as he did. Who was I to tell him what he could or couldn't do?

I willed my own voice to work so he could hear my honest reply. I nodded, agreeing with him. Yes. I could see it. "It's beautiful."

With the smile that broke over his face, you would have thought I said he'd just won the secret to eternal happiness.

"Let's go find the kitchen," he said. "I think it's through here."

I followed him across the chapel and out through the other door. The hallway on this far side was lit up by a few windows. I followed behind him, my hand on his back to make sure he knew I was behind him. Since I was so close, I could breathe in that sweet fragrance he wore, like vanilla and sugar.

He stopped and opened the door to what was the kitchen. He tried the light switch, only when he flicked it, nothing happened.

"There must be a breaker down," he said. "Want to stay here? I think I know where it is."

I nodded. He went off looking for the breaker box and I stepped into the kitchen. There wasn't much I could see, the window on the other side was covered with a thick curtain.

I crossed the room, being careful as I couldn't really see the floor. The window was high up above the counter. If I was going to reach it, I had to climb on top.

I put my palms on the flat top, pushing myself up. It took some effort because the counter was pretty high for my size. I managed to swing a leg over and get up on my knees. I felt for the wall, using it to steady myself as I stood up. I reached for the curtain, grabbing the edge of it and I tried pulling it aside. It was tacked along the edges. I blew out a breath, placed both hands on the curtain and yanked as hard as I could.

"What the hell are you doing in here?"

The voice was deep, demanding, with an edge that caused me to jump at the same time I was ripping. The curtain fell away from the wall.

I fell backward into the dark.

$\mathcal{N}$ORTH

$\mathcal{I}$ teetered on the edge of the counter, my arms flailing. I only had a split second to move and I was ready to twist my body so I landed on my hands and knees rather than my back.

Hands grabbed me by the hips, stopping me, then picked me up into the air and put me down on the floor. I staggered at the suddenness, but arms went around me to hold me steady.

I blinked rapidly. The sun was now coming in through the revealed window. It beamed into my eyes. His face was in shadow, but I could see he had dark hair. The light left him in a halo glow. He was tall, not as tall as Silas, but almost. He had wide shoulders. I could see a gold circle earring in his left lobe.

"Are you hurt?" he asked. The tone was still sharp, bold, and deep.

I shook my head rapidly. I was too paralyzed by fear to feel if anything did hurt.

He started to let go of me and moved until we were both standing beside each other, the sun light shining over our faces. His eyes were dark, his brows thick, and his jaw broad. His skin was tan. His face had coarse hair from a day or two of not shaving.

Whatever I had thought about Silas being the person I wouldn't want to meet in a dark alley at night, this person was exactly that, only he could scare me in broad daylight.

"Who are you?" he asked. His booming voice radiated

the same power as his intense brown eyes on me.

"I'm..." My voice box squeaked. "I'm Sang."

His face softened but it looked like he wasn't sure if he wanted to believe me yet. "How did you get in here?"

"Luke let me in."

His lips pursed. Was he mad at me? Maybe I should have gone with Luke for the breaker box.

The overhead lights above us turned on. They were dim, but revealed the large expanse of black and white tile on the floor. Most of the tiles were cracked and there were a few missing completely. There was a collection of old mops and brooms covered in cobwebs in the corner. The yellow Formica counter tops went around the entire room, leaving a large space in the middle. There was a normal-sized fridge sitting open and empty, a single stove, and a double sided sink in the middle. There was plenty of counter space, but I knew no one could run a diner with just one fridge and one oven.

I turned back to the guy, who was looking me over. His eyes went from my hips up to my eyes again. "Sorry I scared you. I'm North." He was wearing black jeans and boots with a plain black t-shirt. There was a cord around his neck, dangling from it was something in Japanese that I didn't understand.

"Luke's brother?" I didn't mean to sound like I hadn't heard of him, only he didn't look anything like his brother.

"We're step brothers," he said. "We're still family."

I nodded. "No, I get it. I just..." I felt like I was fumbling. His eyes were so intense, it made my knees shake. "He told me about the diner. I think it'll be great."

"My brother has unrealistic ideas," he said, turning around and walking toward the stove. He bent over, opening the door to it and checked the inside.

I stepped up behind him, looking in from behind his shoulder. The oven had a layer of ashes at the bottom. "It could be fixed up," I said.

"It'll take a lot of work."

"But once it's done..."

He let go of the oven door and it closed with a bang. I leapt back, holding a hand to my chest.

He turned to look at me. "It might not work. Most restaurants fail within a year."

I wasn't sure how to respond. His face was so serious. His eyes held mine. Did he want me to agree with him? To say that there was no hope?

"A good one can stay open for a long time," I said softly, my fingers lightly touching the base of my neck. "I suppose it depends on how good the food is."

He blinked at me. "My uncle's the best."

"Then what are you worried about? People will taste how good it is and they'll love it. I mean, if you work hard and put your heart into it, who wouldn't love it?"

His head tilted back sharply and he squished his lips together.

"Hey! You found her," Luke's voice drifted in behind me. I turned to see him coming in, the smile still on his face. How different he was from his brother amazed me. "What happened to the curtain?"

"She broke it," North said.

"I'm sorry," I said. "I didn't mean to."

North blinked at me again, looking perplexed as to how to accept my apology. "It's no big deal," he said in a quieter tone. "Just be more careful next time."

"I like it like that," Luke said. "I wouldn't want anything blocking the natural light."

Having Luke back in the room eased the tension. I felt my heart calming down a little, but I still felt my skin tingling as North continued to shoot glances in my direction.

The phone in my pocket vibrated to life. I had forgotten all about it. I pulled it from my pocket and looked at it.

"Who is it?" Luke asked.

I wondered how much the two of them knew about me and my situation. "It's Kota. He's wondering if I can come over."

"We should go talk to him," Luke said to North. "There's not much else to do here. We'll have to start with cleaning it up."

"We need to take a few walls down," North said. "We probably should gut the place before we spend too much time sweeping the floor."

"Yeah," Luke said, sounding excited. He pumped a fist in the air. "Let's break some walls." He started out of the kitchen.

North rolled his eyes and followed.

I poked at the phone to let Kota know North and Luke were with me and we'd be there in a second.

We found our way out of the building. There was a motorcycle parked near the jungle gym. It looked like the bike had been a custom job. I didn't see a logo.

"Is that yours?" I asked North.

A dark eyebrow lifted. "Uh huh."

"Take her for a ride," Luke said. "I'll walk."

"What?" I blushed. "You mean, you'd let me?"

North looked uncomfortable. His hand lifted to the back of his neck, rubbing. "If you want..."

I smiled, nodding. I'd never been on a motorcycle before.

The corner of North's mouth went up a little. It was so slight but it softened his scary face. Just a twinge. When he did it, he was actually really handsome.

Luke smoothed a lock of blond hair from his face and shoved it behind his ear. "I'll turn the lights out and lock up." He turned back to the church, disappearing behind the door.

North headed toward his bike. I followed behind him. He stopped short and turned to me. "You'll have to hang on to me," he said.

"Is that bad?" I asked, not understanding.

His lips twisted and he shook his head. "I was just warning you."

"Why?"

Again he seemed confused by my response. I felt like an

idiot. I had no idea how to talk to people. He said nothing, but moved to the bike and then got on it, kicking back the stand and balancing the bike between his legs. "Come on," he said, holding his hand out.

He instructed me on how to get on the bike. I dropped my hand into his. Compared to my hand, his was massive, but also warm and, in a way, I felt safe that it was him driving. I slid onto the seat behind him. It felt awkward because I was wearing the skirt, but the material became tight against my butt as I sat, and it wasn't going to fan out.

"Wrap your arms around my waist."

I blushed, but felt with my hands around his stomach. My palms pressed up to his abdomen. I could feel his smooth, strong body through the material of his t-shirt. When I leaned in to press my stomach and chest to his back, I could smell a light, musk scent. It tingled my nose when I inhaled, warming me. My stomach flipped and my nerves jumped. Touching was difficult.

"Hang on," he said, and he started the bike, the engine roaring to life.

The vibration rattled right to my bones. My fingers dug a little into his stomach, but I tried not to claw him with my fingernails. He felt so big in front of me. My face pressed below his shoulder blades.

He turned the bike in the lot. I hung on with my legs and he took off. Unable to see around him, I could only see to the left or right as we passed by the homes. The strands of hair near my ears flew out behind me. When he neared the bend in the road, my grip on his stomach slipped as he angled his body. I wasn't prepared for it.

He moved one hand away from the handle of the bike, grabbing my hand. He pulled it in front of him until he had my palm pressed to his chest. He kept his hand covering mine for a second and then let go to make the turn into Kota's driveway.

My heart was pounding as he shut off the bike and it leaned as he stepped to hold it up.

"Swing your leg around to get off."

I did, probably revealing way too much leg from my skirt to do so. I used his arm to hang on to until I was standing, and then let go.

He got off the bike, putting the stand into place. He turned to me. "You okay?"

"My legs are tingly."

He smirked. The sight of his lips like that made my heart stop. "Mine, too."

♥♥♥

I sat on Kota's bed with my ankles crossed, the only place I thought I could really sit, with the skirt I was wearing. North sat next to me, so close, I could feel the warmth of his side on my arm. He leaned back a little. I couldn't see as I was too nervous to look, but it felt like his arm had crossed behind me and part of it was very close to nearly supporting my back.

Kota and Luke sat on the floor. Luke was sitting near my feet, almost on top of my right foot. Luke just finished filling Kota in on what they were planning with the diner.

Kota seemed particularly interested in this, asking a lot of questions about capital and marketing plans. "It sounds like your uncle has it figured out," he said, sliding his glasses up his nose. "I suppose you'll ask the rest of us to fill in shifts."

Luke beamed. "So you think it will work?"

The question surprised me. Were they seeking his approval?

"You know it means working during the school year. Are you going to keep up with classes?"

Luke nodded fervently. "No problem."

Kota looked at North. "What about you?"

North shrugged. I felt his arm push gently at my back as he did. "It's the usual."

Kota's mouth dipped in the corner. "I mean it. I don't care if you think you know more than the teacher. This isn't like..." Kota glanced at me and then back to North. "Don't go falling asleep during class, even if you know all the answers."

"I'll keep up," North said.

Kota seemed pleased with this. It was as if the whole thing was settled. I admired the way they looked up to Kota and everything, but this was beyond what I had expected. He was giving them instructions. He was a natural leader, even if he wasn't the biggest or the most aggressive. However, it had me wondering about this group of guys. I just couldn't put my finger on it.

"Well," Kota said. "I'll call Victor and the others to let them in on it."

"Where are they?" I asked.

"Victor and Gabriel are over at the school. It's open today for touring. They're checking it out before registration and the general open house tomorrow. They'll be bringing us a couple of maps."

"It seems like you guys have this down," I said. "It's like you've done this a lot."

"We've been in the same grade since forever," Luke said.

"Since kindergarten," North corrected. "You guys have. I got in late."

"And Silas," Luke said. "I think when he moved here, he got held back a grade. Not his fault. It was just the age difference."

I moved my ankles, switching them around. The action caused me to lean back a little. My back pressed into North's arm. I blushed, sitting up more and mouthed the words, "Oh, sorry."

"Relax," he said. "You can lean against me."

I wasn't sure if I should, but the look on his face left my insides quivering. If I didn't, would it seem like I wasn't comfortable with him? If I did... well it felt strange to me. I relaxed a little, lightly sitting back, feeling his arm steady behind me. When the conversation turned again to schedules, classes and the school, my mind was whirling, totally focused on North's arm. Did that mean he liked me? I wondered what

Luke thought. Were we friends already?

At one point, Luke grabbed at his stomach. "Is it breakfast time yet? I'm hungry."

"We can make breakfast," Kota said. "My mom's gone to work. What do we want? Pancakes?"

"Do you have chocolate chips?" Luke asked, looking at me with a grin.

North caught the look. "My god, not you, too."

"Huh?" I asked.

"Luke's favorite breakfast is chocolate chip pancakes."

My eyes went wide and I turned again to Luke. "Really?"

He grinned, nodding enthusiastically.

North leaned away from me, falling onto his back on the bed. His hands went up to his face, rubbing, his elbows arching in the air. "You two are terrible. You can't have chocolate for breakfast." The edge of his black shirt drifted up slightly on his body, revealing his belly button. There was a line of coarse hair starting from his jeans, making a thin line up to almost where his belly button was. I know I stared for way too long, but I couldn't help it. The sight made my breath catch.

Luke jumped up from the floor. "You can have anything for breakfast," he said. He held out a hand to me. "Let's go cook."

I smiled, reaching out to him. He held my hand as I stood up and then part of the way across the room until we were near the stairs. He let go then, so we weren't tripping over each other on the stairs. Kota came with us, right on my heels. I spotted North getting up from the bed, looking right at me before I moved down the stairs too low for him to see me anymore.

I could have sworn I saw a smile.

♥♥♥

Downstairs, I stood with Luke in the kitchen. I wasn't sure what to do. It wasn't my kitchen.

Kota came up behind us and opened up the pantry. He pulled out a container marked as pancake mix. "Sang, there's butter, milk and eggs in the fridge."

I opened the fridge, peering in. It felt so strange to be looking inside, like I was peeking inside their drawers. I found the milk and other things, collecting them in my arms and bringing them to the counter. Luke found the frying pan and a spatula.

North came downstairs and leaned against the counter with his arms crossed over his chest, observing. "You need protein," he said. "Make some bacon."

"He's right," Kota said. "Sang? Can you grab it?"

I went back to the fridge, checked the drawers, and found the bacon. Luke pulled out another frying pan and flicked on the stove to warm it up.

I pulled bacon apart, waiting for the pan to heat up. Kota found a fork for me and then moved away to start mixing pancake batter. I got left in charge of bacon.

"We'll have to make chocolate chip pancakes part of the diner menu," Luke said. "Like a special." He stood next to me, watching as I released bacon into the heated pan and it started to sizzle.

"We're not serving chocolate chip pancakes," North said.

"Other diners do it," Luke said. "And Sang likes it."

North chuffed.

"You could serve it with fruit," I suggested. "Bananas? Strawberries? That would make it healthy."

"I think we have to build the place first," North said, "before we start planning a menu. Besides, Uncle will make whatever he wants. It'll be his place."

"You're going to work with us, right Sang?" Luke asked, smiling as he lit his burner and slapped butter into the pan so it could melt.

"Um," I started. How could I promise to work when I wasn't sure when I could get out of the house? I looked behind me at Kota, who caught my glance.

"We'll have to see how things work out," Kota said for

me. "I'm sure we can all pitch in when it gets busy."

"I'd like to help," I said, poking at the bacon and then using the fork to flip it over. It was easy to picture working near Luke. He seemed nice. North wasn't so bad, either, I thought. If he cared about Luke, and he clearly did, he wasn't all bad and gruff.

I was about to flip over the last piece when some of the hot grease popped and it caught the underside of my forearm. I sucked through my teeth, mostly out of surprise and pulled the fork away, shaking my arm a little to bring cool air to my skin.

"Easy, Sang," Luke said. "Don't hurt yourself."

I felt a hand on my arm and turned to see North holding me, reaching for the fork. He took it from my grasp. He moved forward, nudging me out of the way, taking over the bacon.

"It's okay," I said. "I can do it."

"Don't worry about it," North said. "Go help Kota."

I blushed, feeling like I got reprimanded. Or maybe not? It wasn't like that. He took over because he didn't want me to get popped again. He was concerned about me. North's face was unreadable, but I was touched.

Kota stirred the pancake mix. When I stepped up beside him, he smiled. "We just need the chips. They're in the pantry," he said to me and nodded to the door at the other end of the kitchen.

I moved to it, finding the chips bag and pulling it off the shelf. Kota was already pouring the batter in the hot pan.

I opened the bag of chips, collecting a handful. When Kota moved out of the way, I sprinkled chocolate chips on top of the batter.

"Yeah," Luke said. "Get a lot in there."

"Don't go crazy," North warned.

Luke shared a conspiratorial grin with me. He leaned in and whispered. "Put extra chocolate chips in his."

"I'll make his a smile face," I said.

Luke's eyes popped open. "Oh! Yeah. Do that."

"I can hear you two," North said. He started plating

bacon and putting more into the pan to cook.

Kota and I stood by while bacon was made and pancakes were flipped. Kota stood so close to me that I felt his warmth from his arm.

He nudged at me. "How's the phone working?"

"Fine." I pulled the pink phone from my front pocket. "I've never..." my voice cracked and I swallowed, patting my throat. "It took getting used to," I whispered.

"You should rest your throat," he said. "You really shouldn't be talking. Do you need some water?"

"What's wrong with her throat?" North asked, his dark eyes fixing on me. "Are you sick?"

I glanced at Kota. His eyes darkened. "Might as well tell them," he said. "They would have found out."

I sighed. Kota put a hand on my back, rubbing softly as I said it as loud as I was able. "My mother made me drink a glass of lemon juice and vinegar." It was easier to say than I thought. It was like Kota's hand on me made me feel brave.

Luke dropped the spatula into the pancakes. He cursed under his breath and then fished it back out.

North appeared stunned. "She forced you?"

I nodded, blushing.

"And it made your throat..." he started to ask but never finished. He fixed his eyes on the bacon. "Shit."

Kota moved away from me and found a glass and grabbed a pitcher of water from the fridge. "Her parents are pretty strict. So that's why we need to text only. No calling her house directly or showing up unexpectedly."

"Why did they make you drink that nasty stuff?" Luke asked softly, plating pancakes. He started spooning more batter into the pan.

I re-opened the bag of chocolate chips and sprinkled smile faces into all of them. "Silas called me on the house phone."

North looked back at me over Luke's head. "That's it? You weren't talking sex or something?"

I blushed, shaking my head and waving my hand in the air. "No, of course not." Why would he ask that? Who did he think I was? "He barely said hello."

"Is your voice going to be okay?" Luke asked.

"She'll be fine," Kota said, holding the glass of water out for me. "It burned her throat but it should heal fully in a few days."

I sipped the water, feeling the coolness relaxing my throat. "It's not so bad right now," I said, using a soft voice so it wouldn't crack and they wouldn't worry. I should have been uncomfortable. After yesterday when they hadn't kicked me out, I was feeling a little unreal around them. What reason did they have to be so supportive and nice to me?

"Is that why she's here?" North asked. He looked directly at Kota. There were looks exchanged between them that I simply couldn't get. The silent communication worked with all seven of them. I studied their expressions, trying to catch on.

"She's here because she's welcome," Kota said bluntly. "She's my friend."

North looked confused. "But she's..."

"I like her," Luke said. He flipped out some more pancakes. "She's got good taste."

I blushed. Were they trying to decide if I should stay or not?

"I'm not questioning your damn choice," North said in a louder voice. "I'm asking if it is safe for her to be here if she's going to get her throat burned out at home. I mean if that happens when someone calls, what happens when they find out she's here alone with us?"

"It's fine," I said. "My mom hardly ever leaves her room. She thinks I spend all day in my bedroom. If I never went downstairs, I wouldn't see them for a week or more." There were times when I went up to my room with apples and crackers and wouldn't leave just to see what happened. The only person that would ever notice was Marie, and she simply didn't care.

North seemed dissatisfied with this. He frowned, twisting his lips as he finished up the bacon. He twisted his neck and I could hear his bones cracking a little as he flexed.

We set the table and sat down to eat. Luke filled my plate with pancakes and North insisted I drink milk instead of orange juice to spare my throat.

Seven guys. Seven friends. It still amazed me how they accepted me so quickly into the group. It was like once Kota said he was my friend, the others were on the same level. When you befriended one, you befriended them all.

After breakfast, I felt my phone buzzing in my pocket.

Nathan: "Are you awake?"

I smiled.

"Who is it?" North asked. He stood next to me as I was leaning against the kitchen counter.

"It's Nathan," I said. "He wants to know if I'm awake."

"Tell him to get his ass over here," North said.

I typed in the message.

Nathan: "I've got training. I can't. I wanted to check in. Have fun. I'll talk to you later."

"What training?" I asked North, who was looking over my shoulder at the message. "Is it for the um... Jujitsu?"

North shrugged. "Probably." His eyes flicked to Kota, who gave the slightest shake of his head.

What did that mean? These secret glances were making me nervous. Was there something they didn't want to tell me? It felt like Nathan was doing something else. He didn't want to tell me about it? I was tempted to text and ask but couldn't imagine the right question. I was a friend, but I wasn't privy to some information yet.

I needed to keep being nice, I told myself. I was just new to the group. Maybe everyone had secrets like me. It was still disappointing. I was sharing a lot of my own secrets with them. Did they not trust me with theirs?

Silas showed up, as promised, that afternoon. Victor and Gabriel called to update us that they finished the school tour and they were going home to take care of stuff, so they wouldn't be around today. There was no word from Nathan, but they didn't seem to be concerned. I thought about sending him a text to say hello and to ask how he was doing at training but the guys kept me so busy, I didn't have a chance.

I was sitting on the couch downstairs. Luke was on my left. Silas was on my right, his arm behind me against the back of the couch. North and Kota were on the floor in front of us. We were watching the roadrunner and the coyote battling it out. I had taken my sandals off and put them by the door. I felt North's hand on my foot. He traced the edge of my small toe. At least I think he was. He was stone still otherwise; I wasn't sure what to do. As it was, Silas's arm warmed my shoulders. I couldn't calm myself down enough to focus on cartoons.

Would I ever feel normal around them and as comfortable as they seemed to be around me?

It made me nervous having Silas there. He didn't say anything about me talking so softly, and I tried my best to be quiet and not give him a reason to ask about my voice. Mostly I didn't want Kota or anyone to tell him what happened. The last thing I wanted was for him to feel bad. If I could save him from that, I would be forever grateful.

We walked Max together. We played a board game. We talked about school. Before I knew it, the time was slipping by and Kota was telling us his mom would be home soon.

"Not that you all can't stay," he said.

"Nuh uh," Luke said, stretching his arms over his head. "Your mom works hard. She deserves to get home and relax. If we're still here, she'd insist on making us dinner."

"That's not a bad thing," Silas said. "I like her cooking."

"So do I," Luke replied. "But I'm thinking that she probably doesn't want four extra people here."

Kota tried to suggest that it was okay, but the decision was made by North this time and Kota didn't push the issue.

We all needed to get ready for registration tomorrow anyway.

North and Luke left first on North's motorcycle. Luke promised to text me later. Kota and Silas walked with me outside. We stood together, just inside of the garage, looking out at the street.

"Will we be able to approach you at registration?" Kota asked. "What would your dad think if we were talking?"

I flicked my eyes at Silas. Did he already know about this part, too? Would he be surprised to hear my mom was so strict? "He'd ask questions. He's not as bad as my mom, but he'd tell her about it. I think it'll be fine since we're in a public place. I mean, I have to go to school. She can't do anything about that."

"You should leave your phone at home," Kota suggested. "We'll be there pretty early. We'll keep someone by the door to watch out for you."

My eyes widened and I looked at Silas. He was leaning against the frame of the garage door, his arms folded, looking serious.

"Why?" I asked. "I mean, not that it isn't nice of you. But you make it sound like I need to be babysat."

Kota smiled. "Have you heard of this school we're going to?"

I shook my head. "It's just a public school, right?"

Kota pushed his glasses up on his nose, his finger remained on the bridge as he talked. "There's over two thousand kids that will be attending this year. Over half are from poor neighborhoods. They've got so many kids, they built trailers in the back for additional classroom space. There's not enough lockers to go around. There's usually only enough for the seniors." He frowned. "The hallways have been known to be pretty unsafe. Fighting breaks out a lot. We were planning on sticking by each other throughout the year. With you here now, we'll have to coordinate carefully. Someone like Silas could handle himself, but I wouldn't want to leave you alone. At least not between classes."

I felt my mouth form an 'o' shape. "That's horrible." I

thought for a moment. "Is that why Gabriel was talking about the private school?"

Both of their heads jerked around so fast to look at me that it surprised me. I felt my eyebrows going up.

"What did Gabriel say?" Kota asked.

I shrugged. "He just mentioned something about a private school he was thinking about maybe attending next year or something like that. He didn't say the name or anything. I wasn't sure if he was serious."

Kota shot a glance at Silas. Silas's face was blank.

"Well he's definitely going to the public school this year," Kota said.

Before I could ask anything else, a car pulled up in the drive. Silas and I walked out of the garage to get out of the way. Kota followed us. Erica pulled her car into the garage. She smiled at us as she got out and waved.

"Are you two leaving? I could make dinner," she offered. Her smile was warm but her face did look tired. She wore a nurse's uniform. Her name tag was still pinned to her chest.

"We can't stay," I said quickly. "We've got registration tomorrow. We should get home and be ready for it."

"Good kids," she said. "Come over sometime this weekend. I'll make cookies. You too, Silas."

Silas nodded to her. "I'll always come over for cookies."

We said goodbye to her and Kota. Kota collected a bag for his mom and disappeared inside with her. Silas and I walked together down the driveway. A dark blue Ford sedan was parked along the street in front of the house. We walked over and stood next to it. I was alone with Silas. My heart was pounding again. I stuffed my hands into the front pocket of my hoodie to hide my rattling fingers. We're friends, I told myself. Friends hang out. I'd been with him all day. Why was I feeling so nervous?

"I like those clothes on you," Silas offered. "It looks sporty. It suits you."

I smiled at the compliment. "Thank you." I wanted to

say something in return but nothing sounded cool enough. He was wearing another pair of jeans and a baseball t-shirt. "What's your favorite team?" I managed to get out.

He looked at me. "For what sport?"

"Baseball."

"Red Sox, mostly. Depends on who's on the team."

"What was up with their pitcher last year? The one from Japan? He played for two games and then they traded him."

His broad mouth turned up at the corner. "You were watching?"

"Not all the time but I catch it every now and again. I'll watch the World Series," I said. "My grandfather used to watch every game."

"Have you ever been to one? A pro game?" Silas asked.

I leaned with my back against the car and fumbled with the phone in my pocket. "Nope."

He smiled. "We should go sometime. Though I think the closest professional team is in Atlanta. Maybe North Carolina."

I felt my lips parting and I was looking at him. Again, I wasn't sure if he was asking me on a date or as friends, or if he was just talking in general. I cursed to myself for being so out of touch with people that I couldn't tell the difference.

"I'd like that," I said. It was all I could think to say.

Silas moved to stand in front of me, the toes of his tennis shoes matched up with mine in my sandals. "Sang?"

I lifted an eyebrow. "Yeah?"

"You're not mad at me, are you?"

My mouth popped open in surprise and I pulled my hand from my pocket to lightly touch the base of my throat. "What for? Why would I be mad at you?"

He shifted on his feet, looking away. The breeze picked up some of the strands of his black hair, and it drifted into his eyes. "I left you alone at the mall. Those guys... If Kota hadn't found you... And then your mom and the vinegar." He huffed and turned away, his hands digging into his pockets. "I'm sorry."

"Silas," I said softly. He knew. Did Kota tell him? They

were best friends since forever, I remembered. Someone told him. I should have realized it would happen. They were honest with each other. Reluctantly, I touched his arm. This is what friends do, right? The move was so awkward for me, I wasn't sure how long I should be doing it. "I'm not mad at you. I'm fine. Really. I'm sorry I didn't tell you about the vinegar. I was worried about you."

He turned his face back to me. He didn't seem surprised by my touch, but he was blushing. "You worried about me?"

I nodded. "After all the trouble I caused at the mall, I was worried you wouldn't like me. I was happy you called. My mother... I can't help what she does and it wasn't your fault. But I'm fine. My voice is fine."

A soft shimmer washed over his eyes. "You thought I wouldn't like you because of that stupid kid?"

I tried to warm my smile up for him although I was shaking from being nervous. "You were nice to me," I said. "Next time I go with you to the mall, I'll stick close by. We shouldn't have left you two alone. I was worried then, too. I thought maybe you'd gotten hurt. We should have stayed and helped you."

He laughed, reaching for my hand that was still touching his arm and gave it a light squeeze. "What would you do in a fight?"

I smirked and tugged my hand but he held strong to me. I tried to playfully punch at him with my other hand to get him to let go. He snatched up my other wrist. He twisted me until my back was pressed up against his chest. With my arms crossed, I was pinned against him. I felt his breath on the back of my head, and his lips moving against my hair.

"Would you know what to do?" he asked me, his deep voice dropping an octave. "If I was someone you didn't know, would you be able to get away?"

I didn't want to get away, I thought. I felt the heat of his body pressed up against me. I was barely tall enough to rest my head against his chest. I did squirm. I pretended to want to be released. While it was warm outside, it didn't matter to me. In my heart, this felt so good, like a warm blanket on a cold day. No, it was much better than a blanket. It left my whole body tingling and feeling alive. My heart was in my ears and thumping loudly. "I'd have to stomp on your feet," I replied.

He chuckled. "Try it."

"No!"

"Why not?"

"I don't want to hurt you, Silas."

His body tensed behind me. I stopped wriggling. We stood together like that for what seemed like an eon in the moment. Slowly he let go of me. I turned to face him. His large brown eyes fixed on mine. His fingers flexed and he reached out toward my face for a moment but stopped short. His arms dropped to his side. He smiled down at me.

"You're not like other girls, Sang."

I frowned softly. How could he say that about me? Did I do something wrong? "I am a girl, though. I know my family is a little weird but I'm normal enough." I was lying through my teeth. I didn't feel normal at all. I just desperately wanted to be like everyone else. I didn't want parents who were agoraphobic. I was doing my best to be as average as everyone else so I could be accepted. Was I failing?

"You're far from normal," he said quietly.

My eyes went wide. "You think I'm strange?"

"Yeah," he said, blinking at me. "I mean, different."

I scoffed.

"It's not a bad thing."

I shrugged, stuffing my hands into my pocket again. I didn't know what to say to him. He just called me weird. Weird like my family. Weird was what unwanted people were. Weird stopped me from having friends for such a long time.

His brows creased and he blew out a perplexed breath of air. "I have to get going."

"Okay." I was still a little hurt but I was sorry to see him go.

He fished his keys out of his pocket and opened his car door. "I'll see you tomorrow at registration," he said. He got

147

in, started his car and drove off.

I walked home alone.

♥♥♥

That night, the house was fairly quiet. My parents were in bed. Marie's light was off. No one had noticed I was gone all day. I was grateful for it.

I took out what I was going to wear for registration the next day, a light blue skirt and a nicer white blouse that buttoned up in the front and had a soft collar. It was thanks to Gabriel's suggestions and the pictures I sent to him of what was in my closet. He had an opinion about every piece I owned. I had a list, thanks to Kota, of the classes I wanted to take. When there was nothing else to do, I sprawled out on the floor. It was after eleven at night and I still wasn't sleepy. I crawled to the corner of my room near the window, looking through the apps on the phone just to see what was available for free. I didn't want to download anything that would lead to more expenses for the guys.

The phone vibrated in my hand.

Nathan: "Are you awake?"
Sang: "Yes."
Nathan: "Are you in your room?"

The question got me to sit up.

Sang: "Yup."
Nathan: "Your window is the second one from the left?"

Where was this going? And how did he know?

Sang: "If you're facing the house from the street, yes. Above the porch."

I waited for an answer. When nothing came back after a

while I sent another text.

Sang: "Why did you want to know?"

Silence again.

Sang: "Nathan?"

I was just about to give up on him when I heard a gentle tap at my window. It startled me so badly that I jumped sideways, dropping my phone, my head twisting toward the window.

With my light on, I couldn't see if anyone was there. I got up off the floor, approaching it slowly, my hand still on my heart, until I was close enough to where I was blocking the light from the window. At first all I saw was the silhouette. Nathan was kneeling on the roof, looking inside.

I hurried to unlock the window and lifted it. He helped open it from the other side.

I stuck my head out. "What are you doing up here?" I whispered. "How did you get up here?"

"I'm glad to see you, too." He grinned at me, his blue eyes lighting up. "I brought you something."

"It couldn't wait until tomorrow?"

He passed me something soft. I took it from him. He sat on the flat part of the roof while I unraveled it. It was the dark t-shirt with foreign writing on it I had borrowed to wear the day I went swimming.

"I thought you wanted it," he said.

I smiled, touched that he risked breaking his neck to bring it to me. "I didn't win the races. Any of them," I said.

"Consider it a consolation prize. As many times as I won, you'll be sitting next to me in every class all the way through med school."

I held a couple of fingers to my lips to help suppress my giggling. "Until I beat you at another race."

"That's not gonna happen, peanut."

The shirt smelled clean. I smoothed my palm over the

foreign lettering. "What's this shirt say, anyway?"

"It says girls are stupid. Throw rocks at them."

I reached out to punch at what I thought was his arm but he dodged a little and I hit his chest.

"Hey," he said, feigning being hurt when I only barely brushed his chest. "I'm sitting out on a roof, you know."

The house creaked and we both froze. I held my breath, listening. When nothing else happened, I looked at him. His eyes focused on my face.

"I'll go," he whispered. "I just wanted to say hi. I hadn't seen you all day."

"Where were you?"

"I had training."

"Jujitsu?"

His smile was gentle on his face, a contrast to the harshness of his masculine jawline. "Yeah. Jujitsu."

The way he answered me, it felt like it wasn't the whole truth. "All day long?"

"I'm tired," he said. "You should get some sleep. We've got registration tomorrow."

It was late and I didn't want to press him. I bit back my questions. Who was I to pry into his life when I just met him? "I guess I'll see you then."

He nodded and then moved away from the window. He crawled on his hands and feet to the edge. He swung his legs down first and held the roof with his hands. He dropped down out of my view. With my heart in my throat and holding my breath, I waited by the window until I spotted him dashing across the front lawn and out into the street.

Nathan the ninja.

♥

𝒟R. 𝒢REEN

I dreamed of my old school with people I didn't know who had turned into zombies. They chased me. The doors were locked. I was trapped.

The phone woke me that morning. I had forgotten to put it back into the attic. I was in bed with it, and it had slipped to between my stomach and the sheets. I felt it vibrating and it tickled me out of sleep. In my dream, it was a zombie biting.

Silas: "I'm sorry if I made you mad."

It took me a moment to remember what he was talking about.

Sang: "I'm not mad."

Now that I had slept, what I felt before with him seemed stupid. It was wrong of me to get angry with him when from what I remembered of the conversation, he was trying to be nice.

Sang: "Forgive me for being a meanie?"
Silas: "You're not mean, Sang."

I smiled, my heart fluttered and flipped around in my chest.

C. L. Stone

Sang: "You're too nice to me."
Silas: "Ditto."

I took my time in the bathroom later. I showered, shaved my body, dried off, used a blow dryer on my hair and dug out a barrette to pull back locks of hair from my eyes without using the clip. It was Gabriel's suggestion. I wasn't sure why there was such an emphasis on what to wear. It was just registration.

I put on my blue skirt, modest white blouse, and sandals. I had a notebook and a pencil with me; Kota's list was tucked into the notebook, along with the paper that I had filled out for registration. We were supposed to bring it to be approved and entered into a computer.

There was a tall mirror hanging on the inside of my bedroom closet. I checked myself out in my reflection. Dirty blond hair. Green eyes. Light skin. Decent clothes. Average across the board.

Marie opened my bedroom door, letting it swing until the knob hit the wall. "Hey," she said. "Let's go." She was wearing jeans and a t-shirt with sneakers. She had heavy makeup on her face; her eyes looked darker with the eyeliner around them. She picked up makeup leftovers from her friends at her old school and only wore it on rare occasions to save what she could. "You look like you're new to school," she said.

"I am new."

"Yeah, but you look it. And that notebook makes you look like a nerd."

I shrugged. I didn't want to say something about what I thought of her makeup. Sometime in the past few years, we had grown distant. We saw each other. We worked alongside each other. We had argued a lot, too. Mostly our arguments focused on who would do which chores. Eventually it became a general need to simply exist without getting involved in what the other one was doing. The feeling around her was what I imagined a co-worker would feel. Friendly

152

sometimes, but we were just as happy not talking to each other. Why hadn't we bonded like I read of other siblings doing in books? It struck me as odd, but I could only guess we were simply different from each other. Something happened between us I couldn't explain, and we were now so far apart from each other it felt impossible to become what I imagined real sisters were like.

"Get going," she said and she walked out to rush down the stairs.

My dad was waiting for us out in the car. I rarely saw my father unless there was a school event or it was a Sunday. Any other day, he worked and although he made it in time for dinner, I usually skipped dinner. He was tall, lanky and most of the time he was cheery around the family. He had curly dark hair and high cheekbones. When he was around my mother, his posture sagged more and he looked tired.

"Hurry up," he called to us. He waved his big hand at us. "You're going to end up in all the leftover classes."

Marie got in the front passenger side of the small, five-year-old sedan. I climbed into the back. I locked my seat belt in, even though my dad and sister didn't. We rode in silence in the car.

The lot at the school was already full. I wasn't sure we would find a parking space, but there were people pulling into part of the lawn. My dad found a spot near the back.

"Remember where we're parked," he said. "If we have to split up, just come back here."

I fell behind them as we headed toward the side door of the school. It looked about the same size as my old school. Gabriel had been right about it being ugly. The building was two stories, brown, drab, no windows except for a handful along the second floor. The grounds were flat, with only a handful of trees along the border. Square hedges grew along the outside walls between sets of doors. The hedges looked like they needed to be watered three months ago. There was a football practice area off to the left, a baseball diamond and some tennis courts beyond it. Each was well worn with holes in the mesh guards, and the benches looked warped. Beyond that, I could see the trailers Kota had talked about. The number of them amazed me. I counted at least thirty and they extended out from the school. 1 wondered how anyone managed to get from one of those trailers to classes inside on time.

"I don't want a class in a trailer," Marie said. For the moment, I agreed with her on that point.

The entryway was crowded. The off-white tiles inside the doors were cracked and uneven. Students coming and going made it difficult to navigate, and many of them stopped to talk to each other without concern of who they might be blocking. Most of the parents looked tired and were leaning up against the walls and out of the way.

It took five minutes just to get through the side door. I scanned the crowd for one of the guys. I wondered if they expected me to come in through another door.

From what Kota described of how dangerous the school was, I tried to make myself small and uninteresting. None of the other students seemed particularly interested in us. Most were concerned with either getting in line or finding old school friends to talk to. I couldn't imagine a fight breaking out when so many teachers and parents were standing right there.

Once we were in the main hallway, the crowd thinned out a little. There were tables lined up near a large glass window that overlooked the central, open-air courtyard. There was one large staircase in the middle of the hallway with parents sitting on the first few steps. Further down the hall, there was a line of vending machines and along the opposite wall was a trophy case. I didn't see any classrooms.

"We'll have to split up," my dad said. "The tables are divided by grade level."

"I'll be fine," I said. "There's my table. You go with Marie."

"He can go with you," she said. Her eyes were on a group of girls crowding around her grade table.

"Fill out your form and come back," Dad said to me. "I'll have to approve and sign it."

I nodded to him. The line to my table was long. I moved to the end of it to wait my turn. I felt a tap on my shoulder and turned around.

"Hey!" Luke called into my opposite ear, scaring me.

I smiled, happy to be found. "You made it."

"I saw you come in. I thought it would be pretty awkward if I just walked up to you."

"I didn't even see you."

"I'm pretty good at stalking girls." He pulled out his cell phone and tapped something in. "We've been waiting for you. I'm letting them know you're here."

Within moments they all appeared. North was in his black clothes, although his shirt was collared, a Gucci logo on the front pocket. Silas had a white collared shirt. Kota wore a white shirt with a green tie. Nathan, Gabriel and Victor wore slacks and different colored Ralph Lauren and Hilfiger polo shirts. To me, they were all dressed a lot nicer than most of the students, who wore ripped jeans, baggy t-shirts and sneakers. I realized Marie was right to wear what she had. She fit in better than I did with the other students. I was glad the guys were there. I didn't feel so out of place with them around.

"It's about time," Victor said to me, frowning. "I've been here for hours."

"I'm sorry," I said. My cheeks heated and I pressed a finger to my lower lip. "Did you all have to wait for me?"

Glances were exchanged. Had it not occurred to them that I'm just one girl? They didn't have to wait. I felt bad enough that any of them were hanging around for me. How much trouble could I get in to today?

"Don't worry about it," Victor said, stuffing his hands into his pockets and shrugging. "We don't have anything better to do today, anyway. I was just tired of standing at the door."

With the boys standing around me, the line was a little crowded. Kota started talking about something with Luke and the others, but over the noise of the crowd, I couldn't hear very well. My eyes shifted to the other students. There was a group of girls not too far away looking at us. One of them glanced my way, her face looking angry and it confused me. I turned away, assuming the look wasn't meant for me. Still, it was intimidating.

"Did you all sign up already?" I asked.

Collective nods. "We won't have schedules until we get them in the mail on Monday. We start Tuesday," Kota said.

"It's all a big pain in the ass," Nathan said and then grumbled something under his breath that I couldn't understand.

"You'll have to watch your language," Kota warned. "School might not have started yet, but the rules still apply."

Nathan rolled his eyes, but didn't argue the point.

"We'll get out of this line. We're too big of a group," Kota said. "Who's staying with her?"

They all said "me" at once. I laughed, but when they looked at me as if they didn't understand why I was laughing, I stopped short.

"Victor and Silas, you stay here. North and Luke, go tail her sister. Just keep your distance. I don't want to scare her. The rest of us will head out to that courtyard. Sang, when you're done, we'll meet out there and then take a tour together."

They were going to keep an eye on my sister, too? I blushed, not having thought of that. Again I admired the way Kota took charge of the group. Nothing was argued over. When Kota made a decision, they simply fell in line.

Victor and Silas stayed by my side while the rest disappeared into the crowd.

"What classes were you getting again?" Victor asked.

I pulled out the paper that Kota had prepared for me and showed it to him.

"You're missing one, you know," he said. "You have to pick seven."

I felt my heart flipping into a panic. "I thought the paper said six."

"You have to pick one more just in case a class got filled up."

I blew out a breath, feeling like grumbling.

"Don't sweat it," Silas said, smoothing fingers through his dark hair, brushing away the locks that fell into his eyes. "Just pick an art class."

I hesitated, unsure of what to pick. My mind went blank as to what other classes there could be.

"What about a music class?" Victor offered.

"Would you be in that one?" I asked.

He frowned. "Probably not. I've got an advanced piano class to take." He wrapped a hand around his opposite arm, rubbing at it. "Yeah, maybe not a music class. No one else takes one."

"I guess the winner is art," I said. "I don't think I can take anything else. I mean, the interesting stuff is reserved for higher grade students."

"What would you want?" Silas asked. "I mean, if there wasn't a grade restriction."

"Hm, maybe a language? Or a writing class? I'm not sure. I wish I'd looked more at the book." I looked at my paper where, before I had met Kota, Japanese and a few other classes had been scribbled in. I had crossed them out to put in Kota's suggestions. My paper already looked like a mess. I supposed it didn't matter. If I ended up in an art class with Gabriel, that wouldn't be bad.

The line was moving. I was going to be next.

"Don't worry about it too much," Silas said, putting a hand on my shoulder. His face tilted to look down at me. "Just fill up with prerequisites. You've got time to learn the stuff you want."

I nodded. It was all I could do. I shared a small smile with him.

"You're up," Victor said. He quickly reached for my hand, and gave it a gentle squeeze. "We'll stand by, out of the way."

My eyes slid to see if my sister or my father were around and had noticed the guys touching me and Victor holding my hand. No one around seemed to notice.

It took twenty minutes working with a school counselor

to line up my classes. I showed her my list and she tried to tell me three AP classes were too many. I insisted it was fine, but she wouldn't listen. She gave me AP English and AP Geometry. After that, she wrote down gym class, the typing class, without asking me, and the general biology class, and then wrote down American history.

"I think I prefer world history," I told her.

"World history is an AP class. You can only have two."

I frowned. This wasn't the lineup I really wanted. I felt uncomfortable that she changed things and that I couldn't confirm with Kota.

She asked if I had alternate choices. I suggested art and she said the art class was already full. I tried to look over the catalog but she got annoyed with me quickly. She wrote in choir and wood shop.

"It won't matter," she said. "You will probably get in your first choices." She handed me the paper with her signature on it. "Go get your parents to sign this. Take it to room 103. It's down the hall and to the left."

The table was surrounded by other students all grumbling that I was taking too long. My cheeks felt hot. Did she have to be so short with me? I scanned for Victor and Silas. I saw Silas's tall frame over the other students. He stood across the hall.

I pointed to my paper in the air and then pointed to where I could see my dad. He nodded to me and then pointed to his own eyes: he'd be watching.

I darted my way past the other students. I found my dad standing by the staircase.

"Marie's done," he said. "She went to the band room to see where it was."

I imagined North and Luke were following her. I wonder if she noticed. "I just need you to sign this." I handed him the paper.

"You already crumpled it," he said. "Two advanced classes?" he looked at me. "Is that okay with you?"

I shrugged. "It's fine. It's all stuff I have to take anyway." My heart was throbbing. I tried to shake it off.

Maybe I was going to get in over my head with too many AP classes. There was nothing to do about it now.

He took a pen from his pocket and scrawled his name at the bottom. "Where do you take this?"

"There's a classroom down the hall I think."

"Get to it. Are you going to tour the building?"

I nodded.

"I'm going to wait in the car. I've got some phone calls to make. Try to keep it short. Find your sister when you're done and head out to the car."

I nodded and watched him go. When was the last time we talked? Before we moved? Even now, when we had time to talk, he walked off to make phone calls. I thought I should be disappointed or sad but I wasn't. I was empty. Strangers in a strange family.

I weaved my way again through the throng of students congregating and talking about classes. I was trying to find my way back to Silas and Victor so they could walk with me.

At some point, I was pushed as some students were goofing around. I ended up pressed up against a man in a brown, corduroy suit. He turned around to look at me. He wore glasses, had brown hair, a bristle mustache and watery eyes. He wore a light brown pair of slacks and an oddly colored orange plaid tie.

"No need to push," he said. His name tag was pinned to the breast of his coat. Vice Principal Mr. McCoy.

"I'm so sorry," I said. I swept my eyes down. "I didn't mean to. It's just crowded in here."

He grumbled. "Kids in a hurry to get into school and the moment you're in, you're doing anything to get out again." He backed himself off and then looked me over. His eyes hovered over the blouse I was wearing and then smoothed down over my waist and to my legs. "You also wear skirts that are too short," he said. "What's your name?"

My eyes widened. I wanted to glance around for Silas but Mr. McCoy stood right in front of me, his arms crossing. He wasn't about to let me escape. "I'm Sang."

"Last name?"

"Sorenson."

"Hm," he said. "Hippies with their names. What kind of mother names her kid Song?"

I bit my lip, too afraid to correct him. My heart thundered. School hadn't started yet and I was already in trouble!

"Your skirt is too short. You're going to have to go home and change. We can't allow students to walk around like this."

My mouth fell open. "I'm almost done," I suggested. "I'll just turn this in and I can..."

"I don't think so." He reached for the sheet of paper in my hands, ripping it from me. He looked at my list of classes. "Choir and typing. How typical."

I bowed my head again, my eyes glassing over with tears. Why was he doing this to me?

"I'll keep this. You tell your parents your clothes aren't appropriate. Go home and change and then come back."

"Mr. McCoy," called a voice. We both turned to where the speaker had called from.

A man approached with sandy blond hair, the gentle curls cut to the middle of his ears. His eyes were a dazzling green and his face was just as kind as his voice. He was a head taller than me with tapered shoulders and a trim body. He had a heart shaped face and appeared young. Maybe 19? It surprised me. I wondered if he was a senior or a recent graduate who stopped by to help with registration day. His wore khaki pants, a white shirt and a green tie, Gucci loafers.

"I was just looking for you, Mr. McCoy." He turned to me, looking down at my face. He used his forefinger to push away a lock of hair that fell in his eyes. "I'm sorry. Am I interrupting?"

"No," Mr. McCoy said. "She's going home to change before she's allowed to register."

I felt my lip trembling. How humiliating.

The man raised an eyebrow at me, looking me over. "And what appears to be the problem?"

"Her skirt is too short."

His lips pursed. "I believe the rule book states that a skirt must be as long as a lady's fingertips when she has her hands pressed to her sides." He motioned to me with a finger. "Miss, would you put your hands to your sides, please?" His tone was so gentle. I wanted to do anything he suggested.

I snapped straight as a rod. My hands pressed neatly to my thighs. I might have scrunched my elbows a little, but even so, my skirt was at least an inch and a half longer than my longest finger.

"It appears she's within regulation," he said.

"I don't think it is appropriate for her to wear it," Mr. McCoy said. His teeth were clenched together.

"Maybe not, but that's not our judgment to make," the man said. He turned to Mr. McCoy. "Is that her registration?"

"Yes, but..."

"I don't see why we have to put the counselors through twice the work. They have enough to do today."

"You know you can't just walk in and take over how I handle these students, Dr. Green. She's not one of your boys." Mr. McCoy barked at him, his fists clenched to his sides.

A doctor? I blinked, disbelieving someone so young had a doctorate.

"I believe we were brought in to assist in any way we can. I think we have enough to worry about with kids who have actually broken the rules than one girl who hasn't." He reached for the paper Mr. McCoy was crumpling in his hands and handed it to me. His green eyes washed over my face, soothing and cheerful. He put a gentle hand on my arm. "I'll show you where to turn that in. You were just heading that way, weren't you?"

I nodded, trying not to look at Mr. McCoy. My heart thundered in my chest both from being so scared and from Dr. Green's hand on me. I wondered for a quick moment if the situation could get any worse. Mr. McCoy would probably remember this.

Dr. Green guided me down the hallway. I was worried the boys would wonder where I had gone or if I'd ditched them. I couldn't simply walk away and look for them.

"I should apologize for Mr. McCoy's behavior," Dr. Green said, his hand still gently on the back of my arm. "I think he means well."

"He's pretty intimidating," I said.

He laughed, his voice smooth and light. "I think that, too. But usually intimidating people feel the same way about us. I think a psychologist would say... well, something boring to young students, I'm sure."

"Something about the worst we see in others is what we actually see in ourselves?"

He smiled, his eyes lighting up. "Well said."

"I hope it doesn't mean Mr. McCoy dislikes my skirt because he doesn't look good in skirts."

Dr. Green's head rocked back, his hand going to his forehead and he laughed loud enough to attract attention from other students. "Now every time I see him, I'll be thinking of him in a skirt."

I smiled. I would, too.

We stopped outside of room 103. The students had thinned out around us. Dr. Green turned to me at the door. He reached out, surprising me, and touched the collar of my shirt. He buttoned it up to the top and then smoothed down the fabric of the collar. "And so you know," he said. "If you wear a short skirt, you should keep your top modest. As a lady, it will make you look more elegant."

His eyes were gentle and he looked up. I knew I was blushing. His smile was so casual and confident. I felt like an idiot near him.

"Shall we go in?" he asked. He held open the door for me.

"Thank you," I said. "I don't mean to keep you."

"It's fine," he said. "I was headed in this direction anyway.

The room was an inner office. There were orange cloth covered chairs, all occupied, and a long orange counter at the far side of the room. There were two secretaries on the other side of the counter who were busy with students.

"Why don't you come with me?" Dr. Green said. "I'll let you cut through this line."

I swallowed, swinging my gaze around, hoping the other students in the room didn't hear. It felt wrong to skip the line. Dr. Green went to a door on the other side of the room, then turned and waited for me. I didn't have much choice, I guess. He was so nice to me. There was no reason for me to turn down his offer.

Silas and Victor will be mad, I thought. There was no way they could follow me now.

♥

Mr. Blackbourne

I followed Dr. Green through a series of small hallways with shaggy orange carpet and painted white bricks. The windowless corridor was dim; only half of the overhead fluorescent lights were turned on. Most of the doors we passed were closed, looking eerily untouched. He stopped at an unmarked door and gave it a gentle knock before opening.

Inside was an inner office with a double set of brown, faux-wood office desks facing each other. Each had a computer and several stacks of papers piled neatly in brown plastic bins. There were a couple of file cabinets in the corners and a cork board nailed to the far wall, with a calendar and some other notes tacked to it. There was a small radio sitting on top of one of the file cabinets. A violin concerto was playing on a low volume.

At the desk against the far wall sat a man who looked similar in age to Dr. Green. His eyes were steel gray, his skin pale like mine. His hair was a soft brown, cut short and brushed back away from his face. He wore black rimmed glasses that were similar in style to Kota's. His face was angular in a way that he could have been a model. His hands were smooth, perfect. His lips were pursed as he looked up, scowling at us. This was not the type of person I ever wanted to disappoint. His eyes alone bore into me in a way that made me shiver through my core. He was as perfect and cold as a polished diamond.

"Dr. Green," he said sharply. "You don't have to knock.

This is your office, too, now."

"Sorry," Dr. Green said, smiling at him and taking a seat at the second desk. The office chair creaked, biting my ears. "Old habit when I see a shut door. Never want to surprise anyone. Besides, the offices here are so small. If anyone were standing behind the door, I'd hit them."

The man across the desk frowned and focused on me. "What are you doing here?"

"Oh, this is Miss Sang Sorenson," Dr. Green raised a hand toward me and then gestured toward the man at the desk. "Miss Sang, this is Mr. Blackbourne."

The name caught in my mind. Could it be the same one Victor had deleted from my phone? "Hello," I said softly, dipping my head in a polite nod.

Mr. Blackbourne's sharp eyes scanned over my outfit and then moved up to my face. "That's wonderful. Now *why* are you here?"

"I am assisting her with getting registered," Dr. Green said. He reached for the paper in my hands. "Shall I help you?"

"She should be outside with the other students," warned Mr. Blackbourne. He swung his eyes at me. "Couldn't you wait in line?"

"She's perfectly capable of doing so," Dr. Green said, shaking his computer mouse to warm up the sleeping monitor. "But she had a run in with Mr. McCoy. I didn't want a good student to be scared away because of him."

"Hm," Mr. Blackbourne chuffed.

"I hope I'm not disturbing you," I said, casting my eyes to the floor, feeling completely awkward.

Mr. Blackbourne said nothing but turned away from me and went back to what he was doing with the papers in his hands, filling them out.

"What have we here?" Dr. Green looked over the paper in his hand. "Now, I can't understand this. Why are all these classes crossed out?

"Well," I said, fiddling with one of the buttons on my blouse. "When I first filled it out, I picked classes that I didn't realize were reserved for upperclassmen. And then the second set some were crossed out because the counselor said I couldn't have more than two AP classes."

Dr. Green made a face, twisting his lips and looking apologetic. "How awful. Does she assume you couldn't do it?"

I shrugged a little. "She just kept saying I wasn't allowed."

"Why have the classes up if you aren't going to let students in them? I tell you, what's wrong with this school?" He turned back to me. "What were your original choices?"

I opened the notebook I had, removing the paper where Kota had written my choices for classes. "I couldn't take Japanese, so I switched to this."

He tilted his head. "Did you write this?" he asked, pointing at the masculine handwriting.

I shook my head.

"Who did?"

I blushed. Did he expect to know? "Kota. A friend of mine."

His eyebrows shot up and out of the corner of my eye, I noticed Mr. Blackbourne looking at us.

"Do you know Kota Lee?" Mr. Blackbourne asked.

I wasn't sure what Kota's last name was. "Dark brown hair? Glasses?"

Mr. Blackbourne sucked in a breath and his gaze fell on Dr. Green. They exchanged some looks. It was so familiar, like how Kota and the others silently communicated to one another.

Dr. Green wrote something on the registration paper. "Do you think you could handle this?"

He handed the paper back to me and I glanced at his choices: Japanese, AP Geometry, AP English, AP World History, AP Biology and the required gym class.

My mouth dropped open. "How do I bypass the restriction? And I'm not allowed in Japanese for at least another year."

Dr. Green leaned in on the desk, propped his head up

with his hand, smiling. "But is that what you want?"

I felt my heart flutter. It sounded so challenging. Yet at the same time, I could see myself getting good grades in all of it. "I want to try."

Mr. Blackbourne looked up from his paperwork and scowled at Dr. Green. "Why are you causing trouble? You don't know anything about this girl."

"I have a good feeling." He held out his hand for the paper and then put it on his desk, signing his name. "Besides, who is going to tell me no?"

I blinked at him. This was really happening?

Mr. Blackbourne glowered, displeased.

Dr. Green started typing and clicking at his computer. I wondered how they seemed to know Kota. This had to be the same Mr. Blackbourne that the boys were trying to keep secret before. Could I ask them about this later? My eyes drifted around the room. A violin melody started up on the radio. My toe tapped to it, trying to remember the name of the song.

Mr. Blackbourne turned to me, bringing a finger to the corner of his glasses and shoving them up his nose. "Do you know this song?"

His question caught me by surprise but I nodded. "It's the song about the swallow, isn't it?"

He nodded, an eyebrow going up.

"But it's the version by Micarelli, isn't it?"

"How do you know it's her?"

"Well, she's got this style. She plays soft. It's hard to explain, but it's different than other violinists. I really like it."

There was a spot on his mouth on the right side that turned up. It was only a millimeter of a difference, but it was all his face required before the sternness disappeared and he seemed pleased. His face was suddenly beautiful. I would almost sell my soul, would do anything, to keep that pleased expression on his face. "Do you like the violin?" he asked.

I fiddled with the button of my blouse again. "I do. I like the piano, too. I think if I had to pick just one to learn, though, the violin would be my first choice."

He fell quiet, looking me over. The moment stretched out. His eyes seemed to be calling out to me, asking things of me that I had no idea how to respond to. No matter how much I wanted to flit my eyes around the room to break the tension, the strength in his stare held my gaze.

"Would you kindly hand over Miss Sorenson's registration paper, Dr. Green," he commanded.

♥♥♥

Seven classes. I walked out of the office with a receipt copy of all of the classes I would be taking for the following school year at this new high school. Seven.

"Most students would have had a study hall," Mr. Blackbourne explained after he adjusted my class list on his computer. "It's worked into a student's schedule. You won't have one." He signed my paper to officially approve the addition and Dr. Green took it back to have it filed properly.

I was going to have a busy year.

I followed the corridor on my way back through to the front of the office area and out into the hallway. The crowds had died down a bit. Most students were already registered; they were just taking a tour. I had no idea where the guys were.

I found the main hallway and then the glass double doors that led to the open courtyard. The courtyard was really a square patch of flat grass in the middle of the school with a few trees and stone benches scattered strategically around. I held the notebook to my chest, looking for the guys.

I spotted Silas's and North's heads peeking above the crowd, across the garden to the left. They were all standing in a circle together. I tiptoed across the grass. Voices were raised in a heated debate. As I got closer, I held back behind Silas where they couldn't see me. I didn't want to interrupt, mostly out of curiosity.

"School hasn't started yet and we already lost her," Luke said. "This is terrible."

"She walked away with Dr. Green. We didn't have a

choice but to back off," Victor said. "We were going to get found out."

"This is bad," Kota said. "No one told them about her, right?"

There was a chorus of "no".

Nathan spoke up, "But why don't we tell them? Why don't we tell her?"

"Maybe this wasn't a good idea," Kota said. It was the first time he sounded doubtful. It surprised me. What were they talking about? It wasn't a good idea to become my friend?

"How are we going to hide it from her forever?" Gabriel asked.

"She needs us," Victor said, his baritone voice dropping an octave.

"We can't take in every stray dog we come across," Nathan replied.

My hand fell over my heart and a gasp escaped me. I slapped a hand over my mouth, but it was too late. North turned and spotted me.

"Sang," he said, his eyes wide open. He reached out to me with a hand, his fingers spread out as if he wanted to grab at me.

I shook my head, taking a couple of steps back. It was hard to breathe or think. The others turned, looking at me, their cheeks all flushing to the same bright red and they all froze. I turned away from them, walking to the door.

"Wait, come back!" Kota called behind me.

I opened the door to the main hallway, running blindly through the crowds of people until I was out in the parking lot.

The unwanted dog.

I had to keep it in until my dad drove us home. When we got there, I locked myself into my room, turning off the light. My pillow quickly became soaked with tears.

They weren't friends with me because they wanted me. They felt sorry for me. They saw my weirdness. They got a glimpse of my family. Now they felt obligated to be nice to me. The conversation they had in the courtyard kept replaying in my mind. My heart burned from the humiliation. A poor dog to feel pity on!

I heard the vibration of the phone in the attic. It was hard to hear unless I held my breath. Over time, I got familiar with what was a text message and which was a phone call. From what I could hear, there were no less than twenty messages and over a dozen attempts to call.

I couldn't bring myself to even look at the thing. It disgusted me that they had wasted their money on someone they didn't even want in their group. What were they thinking? Was it amusing to them to have me hanging around? Was I someone they laughed at when I wasn't there?

And why couldn't I stop thinking about how affectionately they had touched me? Or the way their eyes looked at me? Over and over again, I saw Luke's happiness as he daydreamed about the diner in the chapel, and North's smile after the ride on his bike. I thought of Victor's purchase of Winter, and Silas holding me to his body, of Gabriel doing my hair, Nathan's shirt, and Kota's hands as he held mine.

How naive could I have been? I didn't catch their annoyance or displeasure. How could I have? They were so nice. But they were only pretending. Maybe my mother was right. Being alone and ignoring the outside world was easier to handle.

♥♥♥

I dreamed I ran from a stranger I couldn't see and into an abandoned house. I cowered under the windows as he looked inside and sought me out. I wasn't sure if he would hurt me, but I was afraid if he saw me, he would see who I really was. It scared me to death that he might see me. I didn't want him to know.

That night, when the phone finally silenced and the house was still, I drifted in and out of sleep. When the nightmare was over, it was two a.m. I shook off the dream. It rattled me more than any other I'd had that week. I stood up from my bed in the dark. I had a precise plan in mind. If they didn't like this stray dog, I wouldn't force myself on them. I would never stay where I was unwanted.

I found Nathan's shirt and dug out the phone and the cord. In the darkness, I tiptoed my way down the back stairs and crept through the house until I was at the side door. I opened it and walked out into the night air.

My heart was beating so rapidly, I felt I needed to sink to the ground in order to breathe. I willed myself to continue. I would get rid of these things and it would be over. I could go back to my usual hiding in the shadows, pretending to blend into the wall at school, never having friends and never being normal. I couldn't face anyone like this and be so humiliated.

I hugged the shirt and phone to me. It was so strange how only hours ago I had loved these things so much. They had meant so much to me. The feel of them in my hands now made my chest heavy. I didn't look at the messages. They had made things so clear at school. I didn't want to pretend any more.

I stopped by Kota's house, first. I stood at the end of his driveway in the dark, thinking of what his face would look like when he saw the phone on his front step, messages unchecked. It felt so cruel to do, but I didn't really want to hand it to him. I couldn't face any of them, knowing how they felt. I trusted them all with my secrets. Now I was at risk for being ridiculed at school. The girl with no voice. The girl with crazy parents.

I crossed Kota's driveway. Barking broke through the silence. I paused, having forgotten to mind Max. I hoped he would quiet down again, so I waited.

His barking continued for a minute and stopped short. I looked at the front porch, trying to decide if I should leave the phone there and if I could get there without setting off the dog again.

"Sang?"

I nearly jumped out of my skin. From the darkness, Kota appeared, coming around the house from the back yard. His glasses reflected in the moonlight. He was barefoot, in dark pajama pants and a light colored t-shirt. In a way he appeared to be a ghost. I gulped. I took a step backward, ready to flee down the road back to the sanctuary of my house, where he couldn't follow.

"Wait, Sang," he said, and he broke into a sprint and caught up to me. He had a hand out like he wanted to grab at me but I stepped back again. He held his hands up to show he wasn't going to reach for me again and stood still. "We've been trying to call."

I turned on him, wanting to get it over with. "I came to give this back," I said, unable to keep my voice from shaking. I held out the cell phone to him.

He kept his hands to his sides. "I don't want that," he said softly. "Please, Sang. You don't understand."

"What's there to understand?" I said. My thoughts raced. It was amazing to me that I managed to speak at all. My body shook through to my bones, cold and empty. "You guys don't need me hanging around. I get it. That's fine. I just wish you would have told me."

"We didn't say that," he said. I couldn't see his eyes because of the glare from the streetlight on his glasses, but his mouth was frowning. "You misheard us."

"I'm not a stray dog," I said, my voice rising. I hugged Nathan's shirt to me like a shield, and at the same time, I was disgusted with it. "If you didn't want to be friends, all you had to do was say so. I can go home right now. It doesn't have to be ugly. We'll just pretend we don't know each other. I'm pretty comfortable with being ignored." I held the phone out with one hand away from my body and let go. In that moment, I wanted it to break. I felt broken.

Kota's hand shot out, catching it in the air. His long fingers wrapped around the pink case.

"Next time, stop being so nice." I sniffled, unable to hold in my sobbing that I had thought I had dried out on earlier.

"Sang..." His voice was low, barely above a whisper. His lips moved a little but no words came out.

I turned away from him, sprinting toward the road. Why was he doing this to me? Why wouldn't he just say thanks for bringing the phone back? Thanks for not taking this so personally? Thanks for giving us an out when we were too cowardly to tell you the truth? That you were an unexpected burden?

"Sang!" he called out. I heard his footsteps behind me. I tried to outrun him but he was faster than I was. He reached out, grabbed my arm. I swiveled on my feet, almost falling.

He caught me, his arms circling around my back. He hugged me close to him, his body warming mine. His fingertips massaged along my spine, soothing and strong. I was breathless, a mess from sobbing. I lifted a fist, intending to strike out to him, but I stopped. He was hugging me so tightly, such an intimate touch.

"I'm not letting go," he said. "Not until you hear me out."

I'd never felt such a thing before. Not this. Not a true hug that meant to make me feel better. If I cried in front of my parents, they told me to go to my room and only come out when I got over myself. I pressed my head to his chest, and my tears dampened his shirt. I could hear his heart beating back as powerful as my own. Wisps from his breath tickled my hair. My fingers smoothed out over the material of his t-shirt. How could this feel like he meant it and be a lie at the same time?

We stood silently as he held me for several minutes. I breathed in that now familiar spicy scent. His fingers stroked my back, massaging in small circles against my muscles. I felt his face move and his breath slipped near my ear, warming the lobe. Kota. The most calm. The leader. The first one I'd met. A week ago I was a stranger his dog ran down. Here he was now in this moment, doing something my own parents never did.

"Sang," he whispered softly into my ear. He swallowed and rubbed a palm against my back. "You trusted us with your own secrets. I only wish we could tell you ours."

"Kota..."

He pulled back, moving his hands up slowly until he was cupping my face and I was looking into his green eyes. His tender gaze held me with such affection that I felt my breath escape. "You're amazing, Sang. Ever since I met you, you never once asked about the strange things you saw with us, even when I could see it in your eyes that you wanted to ask. The others could see it, too. You stuck with us. You're so sweet and considerate. We don't want you to leave."

My lip trembled. "But Nathan..."

"Was quoting Mr. Blackbourne," he said. "You misheard him. We once tried to bring another guy into the group, but he found us to be too odd and he left. Mr. Blackbourne warned us that we should be more selective about who we bring in." His thumb crossed my cheek, wiping away a tear. "It was Mr. Blackbourne's words. Not Nathan's."

"But why say it?"

"Nathan was trying to remind us what he would say. He didn't mean it against you. It was a warning to us that Mr. Blackbourne wouldn't be happy."

"With me?"

"With bringing you into the group." He dropped his hands from my face to my shoulders. "We're not just friends," he said. "We're... complicated."

My mind was a complete mess trying to understand him. In my stressed state, I couldn't focus on what he was trying to tell me. He confirmed he knew Mr. Blackbourne. That was a secret before. Why did it need to be? "What do you mean?"

"We're not really normal students," he said. "We go to a different school. A private school." He smiled softly. "Only this year, we're attending the public school. We're on loan from the Academy."

"What's the Academy?"

"It's our school. Well, officially now we're part of the public system. But we'll always belong to the Academy."

Something of what he was saying clicked in my head. "Dr. Green and Mr. Blackbourne, too?"

"They're our professors. They're in charge of us. This year we've set up something different, kind of like an exchange program. They take us in to the public school. We set an example for other students and observe, and Dr. Green and Mr. Blackbourne take charge of part of the classrooms to help change part of the curriculum. It's to help the school get more funding, so they can improve things. There's a little more to it but like I said, it's complicated. And classified."

They brought in seven kids and two teachers to a school with over two thousand students? Why did that need to be a secret? It didn't make sense. Still, maybe this was something I didn't quite understand, or that they didn't want me to. Maybe, when I wasn't so distraught, it would make sense to me. I reached with both hands to my face to rub the last tears away from my eyes. "You didn't want to tell me?"

His lips pursed for a moment and his hand lifted up to brush a strand of hair away from my cheek. "I wanted to tell you," he said. "We weren't really supposed to tell anyone. We're supposed to blend in, but not really get close to anyone. We didn't want to risk being overheard or noticed when we had to do something for the Academy."

"But then why did you want to be friends? I mean why bring me into the group now?"

He smiled then, letting go of me and standing back. "Why would you want to be friends with us? We're not exactly normal. When I first met you, I thought you'd assume we were weird and would back off. You stayed. You didn't even have to say it. I could see it in your face. You're such an open book, Sang. And once the others met you... well... that was it. They all agreed they wanted to try."

"You all sounded unsure back at the school."

He nodded, rubbing a hand through his hair. "We can't tell you everything. We've been told to never tell anyone and

175

we didn't want you to find out. We thought it was unfair for you to be with us when you didn't know what you were getting into. It's not that we wouldn't trust you not to tell anyone..."

I shook my head. "I wouldn't."

"I didn't think you would," he said. "But it isn't just us. The Academy requires strict confidence. Something we might accidentally slip to you, if it got out, could damage the school. If you didn't know, you couldn't say anything. We should have trusted you at least to warn you. You should know who you're mixing in with." He sucked in a breath and then blew it out between his lips. "I'm sorry about that. I want you with us. The others want you with us. We have to ask you the biggest favor in exchange. We're required by the Academy to keep some secrets. You can't ask us to tell you. Could you stay with us even if you knew we were keeping something from you?"

We stood in the street together. My eyes drifted to the quiet houses, where people were sleeping. I could see Nathan's home not far away, a light still on somewhere. Kota's looked so silent, too. How odd I felt about it now. I wanted to belong to this place. I wanted to fit in. How I longed to be normal, and here I was with guys who I thought were exactly that, only to learn that I was completely wrong. In my mind, I tried to think back about what he would consider weird. Was it that their personalities were so different and yet they still hung out with each other? Was it that secret way they communicated? Was it how coordinated they were when it came to everything? I didn't dislike it. What possible secret could a school ask a bunch of teenagers to keep? Why did Kota make it sound so dangerous?

"Will you stay?" Kota asked softly.

What else could I do? This was where I lived. The boys, despite the confusion, had been so nice to me. They weren't normal. They weren't what I was expecting. Why did it just seem like such a natural thing to be around them? Flashes went through my mind of their touches, their smiles and the way they talked to me. Maybe they had secrets. Didn't I have a few? Could I turn them away for being different when I was asking them the same?

A soft smile touched my lips. Why did this feel different than when he had originally asked me to be his friend? Somehow this felt like just the beginning and I didn't fully understand it. I wanted to try, though. I wanted to know. "I'll stay," I said. "As long as I'm wanted."

His lips curled into a gentle smile. "Always."

"Kota?" a voice called from up the road. We turned to see Nathan jogging up to us. He was barefoot and wore no shirt, just a pair of shorts. He slowed when he saw me. "Sang?"

How did he know we were out here? I started shaking again. I'd ignored them all evening. They must be upset.

Nathan closed the space between us and I thought he was going to say something. Instead, he reached his arms around me and brought me close to him, as Kota had done, in a big hug. I smiled, feeling his strong arms around me. *Friends hug*, I thought. *Get used to it.*

He lifted me up off the ground until my toes dangled. "I'm sorry, Sang," he said. "I didn't mean it."

"I know," I breathed out, unable to get a full amount of air in my lungs as he was squeezing me so tight. "Kota explained it. It's okay."

"I'm just really sorry," he said. His body shuddered and he put me down. His serious face locked on mine. "Don't be mad."

I looked at Kota, pleading with my eyes for help explaining.

Kota smiled at me, knowing exactly what I needed. "Let's go inside," he said. "Sang, will you spend the night again?"

Nathan's mouth fell open. "What? She spent the night with you?"

An hour later, I was wearing a pair of Kota's pajama pants and Nathan's shirt, lying awake in Kota's room, in his bed. Nathan was in the roll-away bed and Kota was in a sleeping bag on the floor. Kota had sent a quick text to the group, letting the others know where I was, and that everything was okay.

The replies back were numerous, but Kota told them all to come by in the morning.

"We have a lot to talk about," Kota said to me as he relaxed on his side on the floor. "I'm sure you have questions. I can't promise I can answer them all."

I did have a lot to ask. The Academy made them keep secrets. They were best friends. If I wanted to be a part of it, to get them to trust me, I had to earn it. I wanted to know their secrets. I wanted to be accepted as one of them.

It could wait though.

I had friends that wanted me. For now, it was enough.

Update Report:

> Silas Korba: Enrolled
> Lucian Taylor: Enrolled
> North Taylor: Enrolled
> Dakota Lee: Enrolled
> Victor Morgan: Enrolled
> Gabriel Coleman: Enrolled
> Nathan Griffin: Enrolled

Notes from Green

Enrolled without a hitch! Principal Hendricks again thanked us for our participation. Cameras are set up securely in various classrooms, in the hallways and within the inner offices. Still trying to insert one in Mr. McCoy's office.

Further note: I'll be taking on an additional student to my experimental Japanese class for the school. Have the secretary prepare a dossier for a Miss Sang Sorenson.

Notes from Blackbourne

Please have the secretary send a copy of the search results of Sang Sorenson to me. Nothing further to report.

For new release and exclusive Academy and
C. L. Stone information sign up here:
http://clstonebooks.com/the-academy-books/

Connect with C. L. Stone online
Twitter: http://twitter.com/CLStoneX
Facebook: http://www.facebook.com/clstonex

If you enjoyed reading *The Academy Introductions*, let me know.

Review it: at your favorite retailer
and/or Goodreads

Books by C. L. Stone

The Academy Ghost Bird Series:
Introductions
First Days
Friends vs. Family
Forgiveness and Permission
Drop of Doubt
Push and Shove
House of Korba (October 2014)

The Academy Scarab Beetle Series
Thief
Liar (August 2014)

Other C. L. Stone Books:
Spice God
Smoking Gun

READ AN EXCERPT FROM THE NEXT
BOOK IN THE ACADEMY SERIES

The Academy

The Ghost Bird Series

First Days

♥

Book Two

♥

Written by C. L. Stone
Published by
Arcato Publishing

♥

$\mathscr{F}$OLLOWING $\mathscr{T}$HE $\mathscr{L}$EADER

That Monday morning in August in South Carolina was scorching. I was grateful for the shade of the front porch and the sweet coolness of the concrete on my bare legs. I stared down the mailbox, urging the postman to hurry.

It was the day before the beginning of school. I had an unusual affinity for classrooms and homework and being among other people my own age. It meant I could watch how they interacted and try to understand reality, normalcy.

This year would be different.

A wasp hovered in the hydrangea bushes along the front of the porch. I ducked my head as it flew past my ear and beyond, toward the neighbor's yard.

The mailman's truck meandered up to the box. The moments ticked by and I could see him fiddling with a collection of envelopes through the window. I crouched below the barrier of the porch and out of sight. I prepped my knees to get ready to run.

The glass door swung open behind me. "Is that the mail?" Marie asked. My older sister stepped out on to the porch. Her angular eyes squinted at the crisp morning sunlight. Her brown hair was pulled back into a ponytail that hung at her neck, the strands reaching down midway on her back. Her t-shirt advertised a marathon she'd never participated in. Her jeans were long, covering most of her feet except for her toes.

I couldn't understand how she could wear so much clothing, but I didn't really expect her to stay outside for long. I thought of how different we looked. I had dirty blond hair, or chameleon hair as Gabriel liked to remind me. He said it changed color depending on the lighting. With my cut off blue jean shorts and a thin pink blouse, I was barely tolerating the humidity.

I turned again to refocus on the mailman. I could still make it.

In that instant, the mailman pulled away from the mailbox for the next one down the street.

I flew off the top of the porch stairs, landing hard on the small sidewalk path that wound around the house and sprinted across the yard. I was halfway across before Marie managed to make it off the porch. When it was clear I was going to get there first, she stopped her pursuit.

I pulled out all the mail, shuffling through bills and junk mail to find an envelope with my name on it. The orange emblem of Ashley Waters High School was printed in the corner. I held on to it, crossing the yard at a slower pace. My heart was pounding from both the running and the thrill of what I held in my hands. A new school, a fresh start, and this time I had an advantage. This year, I wouldn't be alone.

"Hand it over," Marie said, meeting me halfway in the yard.

I removed my envelope out of the pile and gave her the rest. She took the cluster of mail and headed back into the house. If she had gotten to it first, she would have kept my envelope and, more than likely, given it to our mother and I would have had to fight with her to get it back.

I remained in the yard, waiting for my sister to disappear. When the front door closed behind her, I spun on my bare feet and sprinted down the street to Kota's house.

I couldn't let my sister know where I was going. My family couldn't learn my secret. Not yet.

The boys were waiting for me.

♥♥♥

Kota's black rimmed glasses were sliding down his nose a little as he was checking the mail. I called to him from up the road. He looked up and waved to me, pushing his glasses up his nose with his forefinger, masking his exquisite green eyes. "Did you get it?" he asked.

Dakota Lee and I have a tender friendship. Randomly a week ago he brought me into his circle of friends. It was how I came to learn about the Academy, the secret school they held loyalties to. The only problem was, I didn't know a thing about it, and I wasn't allowed to ask questions. I was going to keep this promise for the sake of our friendship, and for what Kota said was my own safety. There were dangers around them that I wasn't privy to. I simply had to have faith when they told me to trust them. It seemed surreal to me, but I kept my mouth shut and my eyes open, hoping to glean, over time, the answers to the questions that buzzed through my head every time they shared a glance or whispered something around me. They were my first friends. My only friends. What else could I do?

I held up my envelope. "Anyone else?" I asked.

"I'm still waiting to hear from Victor and Gabriel. They're heading over as soon as Victor confirms." He flicked through the mail in his hands, pulling out an envelope similar to the one I held on my hands.

"Hey!" There was a shout from up the street. Nathan jogged toward us. He was wearing dark running pants and a red tank shirt with a Nike swoosh on the front. I admired the way his biceps flexed as he held up his envelope. "Let's check them out."

Kota tilted his head toward the house, inviting us to follow. We entered through the side door in the garage. Kota dropped the rest of the mail off in a bin near the kitchen. Nathan held open a door in the hallway, revealing a set of blue carpeted stairs. Nathan held his hand out, ushering me to enter. I padded my way up the steps to the room over the garage, Kota's bedroom.

Nathan dropped onto his knees on the blue carpet and started to rip open his envelope. I sat cross-legged next to him, doing the same. Kota went to his desk, grabbing a silver letter opener and cut through his envelope, unfolding the printout inside. I swallowed as I read my schedule for the upcoming year.

> Homeroom Room 135
> AP English - Trailer 10 - Ms. Johnson
> AP Geometry - Room 220 - Ms. Smith
> Violin - Music Room B - Mr. Blackbourne
> AP World History - Trailer 32 - Mr. Morris
> Lunch
> AP Biology - Room 107B - Mr. Gerald
> Japanese - Room 212 - Dr. Green
> Gym - Gymnasium - Mrs. French

Seven classes. Barely room to breathe. Now looking at it and thinking ahead to the upcoming year, it seemed overwhelming. Maybe it had been a mistake to be so enthusiastic about this.

"What's wrong, Sang?" Nathan asked. His head tilted in my direction, a rusty brown eyebrow arching.

I pursed my lips, twisting them slightly. "I was just wondering if this was a good idea."

Kota looked up from his paper, coming over to kneel next to me and sitting back on his heels on the floor. "May I see?"

I handed it to him. Our fingers brushed as he took it from my hands, but he didn't seem to notice. None of them ever seemed to notice touching as much as I did. If they grabbed my hand or bumped my hip, they passed it off as if it were nothing. Coming from a family that never touched, there was a lot to get used to around my new friends.

Kota's eyes scanned my schedule, reading off the list under his breath.

Nathan got up, peering over Kota's shoulder. "Holy

shit," he said. "How'd you get seven?"

"She doesn't have a study hall." Kota pointed to the paper, lifted a brow and then looked up at me. "How did you get into the Japanese class? When did you meet Mr. Blackbourne?"

Nathan's eyes widened in surprise and looked at me, waiting for me to respond.

I blushed. After everything that happened, I'd forgotten to tell them. "I... well when Dr. Green stopped me in the hall at registration, he brought me to his office. Mr. Blackbourne was in there. They adjusted my schedule."

Nathan and Kota shared a look between them. The only thing I caught was Nathan's eyes narrowing. Did they not like this? It was hard to understand their expressions.

"What?" I asked. "I know it's a lot but you said they were there to help out the school. Is it bad they changed it?"

"No, it isn't bad," Kota said, maybe a little too quickly. "Did you happen to mention us at the time?"

I pushed my forefinger to my lower lip, pushing it toward my teeth. "I might have said something like I knew you, Kota. I didn't say anything about the others. Dr. Green recognized your handwriting on my paper."

"I didn't know Mr. Blackbourne was teaching a class," Nathan said.

"I don't think it was pre-planned," Kota said. He hooked a couple of fingers into the collar of his shirt and tugged.

"What's wrong?" I asked. The way they were reacting to this made my heart shiver. "Mr. Blackbourne asked if I was interested and he offered to teach me. Should I drop the class?"

"It's just odd that he'd take an interest," Nathan said.

"Not fully," Kota said, relaxing into a smile. He handed my schedule back to me. "It's fine. He knows what he's doing. If he wants to teach you, you're in good hands."

Last time Mr. Blackbourne was mentioned, they diverted. Now they seemed nervous. They may not have voiced their opinion, but I got the feeling they didn't want Mr. Blackbourne to know about me, or me about Mr.

Blackbourne. Academy secrets. I scanned my schedule. "I'll still share classes with you all, right?

"You're in my English class," Kota said.

Nathan moved closer to me and held his paper next to mine. He was close enough that I was breathing in the scent of cypress and leather. I tried to focus and compare.

"Just geometry and gym," I said. "But in gym the boys and girls are separated aren't they?"

"We'll mix up sometimes, I bet. Besides, we're all in the same gym. I'll wave to you. Maybe."

Kota's phone rang on his desk and he answered it. After a few minutes he hung up. "All schedules are accounted for. They're heading in now."

Nathan's blue eyes locked with mine. His reddish brown hair was a little mussed but I found it to be charming. He grumbled. "And so it starts..."

♥♥♥

I used Kota's restroom as the guys went downstairs to wait on the others. I adjusted my cut offs a little lower on my hips and pressed my hands to smooth out my blouse, pulling out the lower hem so the length fell over the pockets of my shorts. I kept readjusting the buttons on my blouse, buttoning and unbuttoning the collar to figure out what looked better. There were thin spots in the material and I was sure my father bought it at a used clothing shop. The guys always looked so good. I simply couldn't compare. I was combing my fingers quickly through my hair, when I heard a car rolling into the drive. I threw my hair into a twist and clipped it. No time to fiddle with it. The boys were here.

I ran downstairs and out into the living room. Kota held open the front door, pushing his glasses up his nose. In a line came Victor, Luke, Gabriel, North and Silas. While they were all dressed casually, casual for the guys was a different level. Polo shirts, clean slacks, button up shirts with collars. Everything looked new and I spied Hilfiger and Abercrombie logos. It made me feel like a complete slob in my old things. I shifted on my feet on the blue carpet of the living room, my hands going behind my hips to hide any nervous shaking.

The others greeted Kota and Nathan in the hallway. Silas was the first to spot me. Locks of his black hair hung around his eyes and he brushed it aside, smiling at me. He came close, towering over me and pulled from his envelope from his back pocket. "Hey look, they let me in."

I giggled. His smile widened, his clean white teeth a contrast to his olive skin.

We congregated in Kota's living room. I sat in the middle of the couch. North, dressed in black with a single gold hoop earring, sat to my left, Gabriel wearing a bright orange shirt and blue crystal studs in his ears, sat to my right. Their contrasting styles had me glancing from one to the other, pondering how they managed to stay friends when they seemed so different. The others sat on the floor in a circle facing us. It felt strange to be higher up than everyone else but they didn't seem to notice.

I blushed as North casually put an arm behind my shoulders against the couch cushions. I peeked up at his tan face. His dark eyes caught mine quickly and I glanced away. While I knew he wouldn't hurt me, his eyes were so intense, it had my insides vibrating.

"I vote we get bean bag chairs," Luke said. He might have been North's step-brother, but Luke's long, blond hair loosely hung around his shoulders, and his smile was warm and always ready to laugh. He leaned back on his hands as he sat with his legs crossed on the floor. "If we're going to have meetings here, we need something besides the floor."

"We're working on that," Kota said.

North's fingers traced small circles at my shoulder. I glanced at the others to see if they noticed, but they were watching Kota. I tried not to blush. This was normal, right? I told myself he was just being friendly, and willed my heart to still.

"Now that we have schedules, let's start at the beginning," Kota said, getting the attention of everyone in the

7

room quickly. "Or rather, let's start with getting there."

"I've got Gabriel," said Victor, fiddling with the silver medallion at his neck.

"We're good," North said. "Luke and I can grab Silas."

"Good. Logically, I'll take Nathan and Sang," Kota said.

"You mean on the bus?" I asked. They all looked at me. I felt my cheeks radiating heat. "I mean, I don't think I could get away with riding to school with anyone. If I'm not getting on the bus, my sister will know and she'd tell my parents."

"Aw, shit," Nathan said. "I didn't think about that. Don't tell me we're riding this year."

I held up my hand toward him. "You don't have to. I mean, I can ride the bus. You guys can ride together. It's no big deal. I'll just see you when I get there."

The group exchanged glances. I caught Luke's gaze as he stared at me, his blond hair falling in front of his dark eyes. I wasn't sure if he realized he was doing it, or maybe he was just staring out into space but happened to be looking in my direction. When he came back, he started blinking his brown eyes and held a dazzling smile. His striking face had distracted me from watching the others. Did he do that on purpose?

"It's not a big deal," Nathan said, falling back on the carpet, putting his hands behind his head to prop it up. "We'll do it."

"But," I started to say. It just seemed too unfair. It wasn't a big deal to me. It was just a bus ride.

Kota cut me off. "No, it's fine. My car isn't totally reliable anyway. We'll ride."

I pursed my lips. His easy excuse, to make me feel better, left me feeling uneasy. The others simply nodded, taking Kota's lead. When Kota finalized a plan, everyone went through with it. It was hard for me to believe the guy who appeared to be one of the least aggressive; the least likely leader had come to the role he had developed.

"But that brings us to another issue," Kota said. His fingers brushed away the neatly-trimmed brown hair against his forehead. "We need to work on getting your parents used to us. It'll be difficult, but the sooner we find a way, it'll make it easier on all of us."

I bit my tongue to keep from saying something. I'd told him before I liked the way things were working now. My father didn't come home until very late in the evening, often well after eight when I was already up in my room and I didn't see him at all. My mother, who was ill, kept mostly to her room. I checked in once a day, and for the most part, I could escape outside. If she did ask where I had gone, I would rattle off different things; in the woods, the garage, taking a walk to the empty church down the road. In our old neighborhood, back in Illinois, I often took walks outside. Since the closest kid lived a couple of miles away, my mother eventually relaxed to let me walk in the woods near the house. Marie told me they bought our new house here on Sunnyvale Court because it was the least crowded street within an hour's drive of where my dad worked. It was a last minute purchase and my mother wasn't happy about it, but it did have a lot of wooded areas. So far, she hadn't questioned my going for walks. She only reminded me that I shouldn't talk to anyone. My mom would eventually realize how many kids were on this street. I didn't want to think about the restrictions she would impose once she found out. I needed to be more careful, though. I had to show up more around the house on occasion.

Gabriel reached out to my head, rubbing at my hair. I held back from cringing out of fear. I enjoyed their touches but they were always so unexpected and when they did it quickly, my first reaction was usually to back up as I was always sure they didn't mean to or it was an accident. "Don't worry," he said, his thin fingers massaging my scalp. "We've got a plan." He let go of me and turned his head to Kota. "We've got a plan, right?"

Kota brushed his own fingers through his hair "I still think we ought to call on Danielle. If we can get them to be friends, she could invite Danielle over. Her mother might get used to another girl being over there easier and we could slowly start showing up."

There was a collective groan.

"Is she that bad?" I asked.

"Yup," North said, his voice deep. His fingers stopped the gentle motion at my shoulder and simply rested against me. It wasn't exactly that he had his arm around me. It just felt like two fingers touching me. I kept telling myself to cool off. Would my heart always pound so much around them?

"She's a typical girl," Nathan tried to explain. "She thinks we're all a bunch of nerds."

Gabriel nudged my arm with his and leaned into me to stage whisper near my ear, "Nathan used to have a crush on her."

"Fuck, no, I didn't."

"She used to go over to his house," Gabriel continued. "One day she tried to get him to skinny dip in the pool. When he refused, she got pissed and told everyone he was gay for a while."

"Like I give a shit what she thinks," he said, but he frowned and rolled onto his side on the carpet, covering his eyes with an arm. "Can we not talk about this right now?"

Kota cleared his throat. "Well, maybe something else will come up." He pulled out his schedule and unfolded the paper. "Are we ready?"

It took a good hour between us to get organized. Most of that time was taken up by general talking among the guys and Kota had to remind them what they were trying to do. Kota kept notes on a sheet of paper. In the end, my own schedule was marked up with his writing.

Homeroom Room 135
Luke, North
AP English - Trailer 10 - Ms. Johnson
Kota, Gabriel, Luke
AP Geometry - Room 220 - Ms. Smith
Nathan, North
Violin - Music Room B - Mr. Blackbourne
None

AP World History - Trailer 32 - Mr. Morris
Victor, North
Lunch
AP Biology - Room 107B - Mr. Gerald
Silas
Japanese - Room 212 - Dr. Green
Victor
Gym - Gymnasium - Mrs. French
Gabriel, Nathan

It seemed everyone was in each other's classes, except for their special electives and Kota's advanced science and math classes. I considered it unreal but I wondered if part of the reason was because they were from the Academy. Did Mr. Blackbourne and Dr. Green fix their schedules, too?

By the time we had it sorted out, I was sitting on the floor, leaning against the couch. Gabriel moved across the room and was talking to Luke. North stretched out on the couch. I was quietly reviewing my schedule again, when, out of the corner of my eye, I caught Victor scooting over to sit next to me.

"I already know a little Japanese," Victor said. He sat with his legs crossed and his knee grazed mine. The fire in his eyes flickered. "It's actually pretty easy to speak it."

I tilted my head as I looked at him, trying to ignore his knee pressing against mine. "How did you get in this class? I thought it was for upperclassmen? I had to get special permission from Dr. Green."

"Who do you think let me into his class?" He smiled at me. "He'd let anyone in if they asked, actually."

That confirmed things. If Victor's schedule was altered, the others were most likely done as well. Did that mean Mr. Blackbourne and Dr. Green wanted me in the same classes as the boys? "Where did you learn Japanese?"

"My parents travel a lot. They like to stop in Japan."

My eyes widened. "I'm jealous," I said. "Can you say

something in Japanese?" It wasn't a challenge, but genuine curiosity in his ability.

A smile touched his lips. "*Kirei-na hitomidane*." The way he said it in his baritone voice made it almost sound like a song lyric.

"Kirei..." My lips moved to try to mimic what he said but I lost it half way through. "What does it mean?"

That fire lit up in his eyes and his cheeks tinged red. "I'll tell you later."

I smoothed my fingers over the lower hem of my shorts in a nervous reflex. Did I ask something embarrassing? Did it sound like I didn't believe him? I went with changing the topic since I didn't want to say anything else wrong. "At least we've all got classes together or similar classes. Studying should be easy. Except for Kota."

"Are you going to be okay, Kota?" North asked from behind me. He was on his side, a cushion pillow propped up under his head. He looked half asleep. "There's periods where we won't see you for several hours."

Kota shrugged and waved his hand in the air, dismissing his words. "Most of these classes are close together on the second floor. I won't be in the hallways for very long."

Silas had been completely quiet for a long time, concentrating on his schedule. While the others were busy talking about how to get from one class to another with the trailers being a problem, I crawled over to him. He caught my eye and he patted the spot next to him, indicating I could move in closer.

"We've only got one class together," I said, sitting next to him, holding my paper near his.

He inched over, putting an arm behind me with his palm to the floor. He was close enough that his arm touched my back. "At least I get you to myself," he said, the corner of his mouth lifted up.

My fingers shook because of his touch. I put my paper down so I could hide my hands in my lap. "In a class full of people," I said.

He put his paper in his lap and leaned back on his hands.

"It won't matter if they're there. I don't really talk much."

"Why?"

"Not a lot to say."

"You talk to me."

He reached over, moving a lock of my hair that had slipped away from my clip, tucking it behind my ear. His big fingers brushed across my cheek and against the lobe of my ear. "You talk to me, too."

My heart did flips in my chest.

There was a knock at Kota's door. All of us looked up at the same time toward one another.

"It can't be the mailman," Kota said, his brows creasing. He got up off the floor. As he walked around me toward the door, he dropped a palm on top of my head, pushing slightly to make my head bob down. I looked up just in time to catch his grin before he left the living room. I grinned back. It was nice to feel wanted. I tried to tell myself again that touching was normal among friends. They might be friends with a lot of secrets, but they were normal in their behavior, right? Having missed out on this for so long, I was simply unused to the attention. Did anyone ever get over this feeling or was this fluttering nervousness something they felt all the time?

It was only a minute before Kota returned, we all looked up at him expectantly. He looked pale.

"Kota?" Luke said. "What? Who was it?"

"It's your sister," Kota said, turning to me. "Your older sister. She's asking for you."

My heart stopped. How did she find out? How did she know I was here? My hand fluttered to the base of my throat and I leapt up. I didn't want her coming in. It would be bad enough she knew I was at Kota's. It would be worse if she knew there were seven guys here.

Silas caught my other hand, looking up at me from the floor. "Are you going to be okay?" he asked, giving my hand a gentle squeeze.

I shrugged my shoulders and tried to keep my expression calm. I squeezed his hand back. "Don't worry. It'll be fine." After the last time when my mother had reacted badly when

Silas called, I didn't want to scare him with my worry over what she would do to me. I was too terrified now to be nervous that he was holding my hand.

"Would your sister say you were here?" Kota asked, pushing his glasses up on his face again even after they were already adjusted. I had the feeling it was what he did when he was thinking.

"Maybe," I said. "It might require negotiations." They all looked confused and I waved my hand to them, taking the paper that had my schedule and putting it in my pocket. "I have to go calm the waters. I might not be back today."

"Be careful," Silas said. He squeezed my hand again before letting go. The others looked like they wanted to say something, but no one did. North was sitting up on the couch, his hands clenched. Nathan stared at the floor. Gabriel, Luke and Victor looked between Kota and I, as if waiting for either of us to tell them what to do.

Kota walked with me to the door and the others stayed behind. I wanted to say something more to them, but there wasn't much else to say. This was far beyond what I was prepared to handle at the moment.

Outside, Marie was waiting on the steps. Her hands were in her jean pockets and she was looking impatient and sweating. I stepped out onto the porch. Kota had his hand gently rubbing my back on the way out and pulled it away before Marie could catch it. The instant his hand moved, I felt a loss. His touch was helping me to feel brave.

I stepped away from the door and gave Kota a small wave. He waved back, looking sympathetic. He said nothing but gave me a look that for once I understood. He wanted a word from me the moment I could find a way.

"Mom wants you to go home," Marie said after Kota closed the front door. "She's been asking for you for a couple of hours now."

"How did you know I was here?"

"I took a guess," she said.

I was fuming inside, angry at myself for being so reckless. She must have seen me from the house. "Does mom know I was here?"

Marie shrugged. That didn't mean she didn't know. It was her way of saying she wasn't going to tell me. This was bad. If Marie had gotten into trouble with something, she could have used her knowledge of where I was to try to get herself out of a punishment. It often worked.

We got back to the house and entered through the side garage door. As soon as we were standing in the living room, I heard my mom's voice ringing through the house.

"Sang! Come here now!" The anger and power radiated through her tone and it felt like the house was shaking around me. It was all I needed to hear. She knew everything.

Marie filed off past me and headed toward the stairs. She was getting out of the way. I was going to face this part alone.

The Academy

The Ghost Bird Series

First Days

♥

Book Two

♥

Written by C. L. Stone
Published by
Arcato Publishing

ABOUT C. L. STONE

Certification

- Marvelour of Wonder

- Active Participant of Scary Situations

- Official Member of F.A.M.E.

Experience

Spent an extraordinary number of years with absolutely no control over the capping of imagination, fun, and curiosity. Willingly takes part in impossible problems only to come up with the most ludicrous solution. Due to unfortunate circumstances, will no longer experience feeling on a small spot on my left calf.

Skills

Secret Keeper | Occasion Riser | Barefoot Walker Strange Acceptance | Magic Maker | Restless Reckless | Gravity Defiant | Fairy Tale Reader | Story Maker-Upper | Amusingly Baffled | Comprehensive Curiousness | Usually Unbelievable

58819827R00113

Made in the USA
Columbia, SC
24 May 2019